BICEPS OF DEATH

David Stukas

KENSINGTON BOOKS
http://www.kensingtonbooks.com

KENSINGTON BOOKS are published by

Kensington Publishing Corp.
850 Third Avenue
New York, NY 10022

All Kensington titles, imprints and distributed lines are available at special quantity discounts for bulk purchases for sales promotion, premiums, fund-raising, educational or institutional use.

Special book excerpts or customized printings can also be created to fit specific needs. For details, write or phone the office of the Kensington Special Sales Manager: Kensington Publishing Corp., 850 Third Avenue, New York, NY, 10022. Attn. Special Sales Department. Phone: 1-800-221-2647.

Kensington and the K logo Reg. U.S. Pat. & TM Off.

ISBN 0-7582-0639-9

First Hardcover Printing: September 2004
First Trade Paperback Printing: December 2006
10 9 8 7 6 5 4 3 2 1

Printed in the United States of America

This book is dedicated to Gil Tripp, who never gave up when the going got tough—literally. Put the boots on Gil, and let nothing block your path.

Acknowledgments

To John Scognamiglio, my ever supportive and patient editor; Alison Picard, my agent; and to my copy editor, Joan Matthews, who trembled every time she rewrote something, but still managed to hold her red pencil steady enough to make my book and even better one.

BICEPS OF DEATH

I

Oh Baby, Oh Baby

"PUSH!" Michael hissed through gritted teeth.

"I can't!" I pleaded from a slightly disadvantageous position on my back, legs in the air.

"Push, I'm telling you!" Michael barked. "If you don't push right now, you're going to be sorry."

"It hurts, Michael!" I screamed back.

"C'mon, just arch your back and give it one big thrust!" Michael drilled me.

"I can't take this!" I screamed, begging for mercy. Sweat was rolling down my face and stinging my eyes.

"Listen, keep those legs spread wide! If you don't, you're not going to feel the full force!" Michael said, grabbing my legs and pulling them farther apart.

"Michael . . . I . . . I . . . think I'm . . . I'm going to explode!" I growled, the words rising up from deep inside my gut and rushing out in a torrent. "Ahhhhhhhhhhhhhhh!"

My body convulsed and shuddered as it released a lifetime of tension.

"Four hundred and fifty pounds! I knew you could do it," Michael said triumphantly.

Michael was under the delusion this beautiful Thursday morning in May that my recent dedication to bodybuilding was entirely due to his efforts to "make me see the light" of his theory that in order to get a man, you have to have the right bait. And you can't look like live bait either. You have to have pecs with deep clefts, arms bigger than most people's heads, and thighs that rub against each other as you walk. Forget trying to develop a witty and agile mind, impeccable taste, and a captivating personality—these take too much time to develop, force you to read books, and keep you out of the gym. Michael isn't alone in his thinking, either. It seems that the majority of gay men have swallowed this mode of thinking hook, line, and sinker. You only have to pick up an issue of those free gay rags that have sprouted up in every major city to realize that the cult of the body has taken over the gay world. If you don't have a killer body, then you better capitalize on your offbeat looks or have plenty of money. This line of reasoning takes us into a predicament that will rear its ugly little head in my life soon enough, but we'll get to that in a matter of a few pages. Stay tuned.

While I decided it was best to let Michael think he alone had been the motivation for getting me into the gym, the reason lay three thousand miles to the west in California. Palm Springs, to be exact. Yes, dear readers, Robert Wilsop, professional hand-wringer, obsessive-compulsive, personal doormat, and whipping boy (not literally), had snagged a boyfriend. And not just any boyfriend, but a warm, caring, sensitive, tasteful individual who didn't insist on wearing a ski mask during sex. (I confess, Darrin was exciting at first, but after a while, you get *tired* of being abducted whenever you just want to have sex. I dropped him after he wanted to meet me in a Brooklyn shipyard, throw me in the trunk of his car, and take me to an undisclosed location in upstate New York—call me old-fashioned.)

I got up from the leg press machine to let Michael take his turn. He threw his Frette towel down on the vinyl seat, scribbled in his workout diary made of Crane handmade paper, and proceeded to make a big and loud show of adding a handful of forty-five-pound plates to the machine. I—and everyone else in the gym—was supposed to look on in awe, but no one did. Michael was by no means the biggest guy in the gym.

Michael released the safety catch and the titanic weight stack creaked slowly downward like a marauding tank, but it was no match for Michael's overdeveloped quads, which inflated with a rush of energy and repelled the weights back to their starting point. The battle was over—the weights had lost. Michael did eleven more reps, the blood rising to his face so alarmingly, I waited for his eyes to shoot out of his head.

"Michael!" I exhaled. "Are you sure you should be doing that much weight? It looks dangerous."

"Danger is my middle name," he replied.

"I thought it was Slut."

Michael laughed briefly at his own reputation. "Call me anything you like, but it's because of my good looks and wild reputation that that huge bodybuilder trainer over there can't keep his eyes off me."

"I think he's looking at you because he never saw anyone wearing leather workout shorts before," I commented.

"Aren't they great? They're from Frank Addams. Feel the leather, Robert . . . it's like butter."

Michael grabbed my hand and placed it squarely on his crotch. "Rub your hand over it so you can really feel it. What do you think?"

"I think that mine isn't the only hand that has been there

lately," I responded, making an observation that was no shot in the dark. "Michael, why are there teeth marks on the crotch of your shorts?"

"Where?" he said alarmingly.

"Right there," I said, pointing. "Near the zipper."

"Goddamnit," he complained. "I told Bob to watch his teeth! Oh well, now they're broken in."

"I am not even going to comment on your comment, Michael."

"Yeah, and if I were to have things my way—and I always do—I will have another set of teeth marks on the crotch of these shorts by the end of this workout."

"And whose, pray tell?"

"That big ol' bodybuilder trainer over there," he said, gesturing with his eyes.

Michael placed total confidence in his ability to seduce men—for good reason. He almost always got what he wanted. His talent was unlike any other I had ever seen. Of course, it wasn't just his dark, good looks, his six-foot-one-inch frame that was ripped with muscles, or his piercing blue eyes that reeled the men in. The sizable income he received from his family's pharmaceutical concern helped put him over the top. After all, there's nothing sexy about a muscle god if he can't pick up the tab at an expensive restaurant.

"Oh, did you read in the paper about the trainer who used to work here?" I said.

"No, what happened? His posing strap get lodged up his ass crack?"

"No, it seems that he leapt off the terrace of his thirty-second-floor Madison Avenue apartment."

"Oh my God, is he all right?"

"Yes, Michael, he's nursing a sprained ankle at Cedar Sinai right now."

"Oh, right. Dead, huh?"

"I would hope so," I added. "Wait a minute . . . what's a bodybuilder trainer doing in a Madison Avenue apartment? Do they make that much money training overweight men who want them to do squat thrusts over their face?"

Michael looked at me like I had grown up in the Midwest, a fact to which I plead guilty.

"My God, you're naïve, Robert!" Michael reprimanded me. "Do you think that someone who earns one hundred dollars an hour is going to be able to afford an apartment with a terrace on upper Madison Avenue?"

"Are you suggesting that this guy had a sugar daddy?"

"Jesus, who taught you about life in the big, bad world, Robert?"

"Certainly not my parents. Their motto was: 'Denial as a way of life.' "

"Well, wise up. Most of these trainers make a fantastic side living hustling their clients, acting as escorts, or selling steroids to clients who want to get big really fast. The training bit is just a cover for their other businesses."

My eyes widened as big as Le Creuset saucepans. "Wow" was all I could say. I looked across the gym at a trainer named Eric and saw him in a whole new light. He wasn't just a freakish monster with two snake tattoos winding and climbing up his enormous arms. He was now a cunning steroid spider, beckoning unwitting clients into his web of carnal deceits.

"So you're telling me that Eric over there," I said, pointing discretely at sequoia thighs, "is probably a hustler?"

"Not probably," Michael said, uttering a blast of air and doing a set of leg presses. Puff, puff, puff, puff, puff. "He *is*," he added, finishing his set with a tremendous clank of the weights for all to hear. Still no eyebrows were raised.

"Oh, Michael, how you do know that for sure? I thought he was straight."

"Yeah, straight to bed."

"Really?" I asked.

"I invited him home for sex one day and he had the nerve to try and charge me five hundred dollars an hour."

"Did you pay?"

Michael was aghast. "Why should I pay for something when I can get it for free?"

"Did you say *give* or *get?*"

"Plenty of guys would pay more than five hundred dollars an hour just to sleep with me," Michael boasted.

"Then why don't you?" I answered. "This might solve your chronic shortage of money."

"I can't, Robert. I don't want to look like a whore."

I bit my tongue so hard, I could taste blood. Just let this one go, Robert. Too easy.

"Five hundred dollars an hour, huh?" I wondered out loud.

Michael looked into my face and read it clearly. "Don't even think about it, Robert. You as a hustler? I don't think so. You're so law-abiding, you'd make your clients give you 1099s and report the income."

"Why not become a hustler, Michael? I'd make a lot more than I do in advertising. Plus, it's pretty much the same thing."

Michael gave me a withering glance. "Just remember that you can't sell from an empty pushcart."

"Well, for having nothing for sale, it looks like Eric is giving me a lot of eye."

"No way!" Michael exclaimed.

"See for yourself, Michael."

Michael hopped off the leg press machine and squinted

in Eric's direction. "Well, I'll be. He's probably looking at you because he senses that you'd make a good candidate as a sex-for-pay client."

"Ha, ha. That's weird. Look at his gym bag."

"What's so weird about it, besides the fact that it's made of cheap leather?" Michael asked.

"Look at the way he's holding on to it. You'd think he has a million bucks in there."

"It's probably filled with steroids or human growth hormones. I wonder how much he charges for a thirty-day cycle?"

"Michael! Those things will kill you! Promise me you're not taking steroids again."

"I'm through with those. Right now, I'm on this new stuff—it's a hemodilator. I take four of those twice a day, combined with HMB, creatine, glutamine once a day, androstenediol three times a day, X2 I-don't-know-how-many-times-a-day and a whole bunch of M3, and Metamucil."

"Michael, a meth lab uses fewer chemicals. Do you really think those supplements do any good but line the pockets of the companies who make them?"

Michael was incredulous. "Of course they do! Just look at me!" he said, flexing his biceps for extra emphasis.

"Michael, that's because you have no real job to speak of and you work out seven days a week for two hours a day—even Drew Carey would be buff. Plus, why does everyone that you even deign to talk to have to be VGL—very good looking? Can't you see that if you constantly build your relationships around physical attraction, they end up shallow and short-lived."

"Well, duh-uh! I *want* shallow, short-lived relationships. I'm perfectly happy with my life and my roomy penthouse apartment in the Village. The last thing I want is some guy

moving into my comfortable bachelor life, sharing my underwear drawer, and using my rejuvenating creams."

"Michael, the only time I have ever known you to wear
underwear was when you caught crotch rot from the guy
who worked for the phone company."

"Hey, don't knock him!" Michael warned me. "I broke
several phones just to get this guy to come back and fix
'em."

"Can we get back to the subject at hand?" I implored.
"Er, Eric . . . and the two big guys who just came in," I said,
pointing toward two men who had recently slipped into the
gym and stood watching Eric from the sidelines. The way
they observed Eric, it was clear that they weren't there to
admire his muscles. Plus, the way they were dressed suggested that they were working for the police or some special
tactical division. They had black cargo pants, black T-shirts,
and those special boots you see cops and armored car
money carriers wearing—the ones that the pants were often
tucked into. They leaned against a pillar and stared lazily at
Eric as if they had all the time in the world.

The sudden attention that the two men were paying Eric
had the most profound effect on Mr. Musclehead. He struggled to keep his attention on his client, but he kept looking
over at his watchdogs. In no time, he broke a sweat that I
could see from across the gym where we stood. This couldn't
be good.

"Michael?" I started, looking at my wristwatch grandly.
"Could we end our session a little early? I think my legs
have had it," I said, hoping to get into the locker room, retrieve our gym bags from the lockers, then split before
someone started shooting. I've lived in New York for over a
decade now, but I will never get used to the idea of bullets
entering my body.

For once, Michael agreed to leave a gym without having a gun pointed at his head.

"Might as well . . . no good men here today," he lamented.

"Let's go," I said, grabbing my towel and pushing Michael toward the locker rooms.

"What's with the pushing and the rushing all of a sudden?" Michael exclaimed.

"Later," I hissed through gritted teeth. "I'll tell you later . . . outside."

Michael looked at me as if I had just started eating bugs. "I don't get it," he added.

"Just grab your bag and let's go," I pleaded.

We retrieved our gym bags and were about to leave when a hulking presence blocked our retreat. The appearance of this form looming over us scared the bejesus out of me. It was Eric. He grabbed my gym bag out of my hand, took a CD-ROM jewel case from his own gym bag and tossed it into mine, then returned my bag while I stood there with my jaw wide open.

In a whisper that bordered on softly yelling, he said, "Hold on to this, I'll be back to retrieve it . . . later!" He and his precious gym bag headed toward the emergency exit, pushing the door open and causing the unhappy door to wail in alarm. Michael and I left the gym, noticing that the two imposing men were nowhere to be seen.

As we descended in the elevator to the street level, Michael pawed at my gym bag several times, prompting me to slap his hand away each time.

"Michael, let's get clear of the building before we look at what Eric gave me," I explained. "I don't want those goons to see that I have something they might be looking for."

"I don't get it," Michael reported. "What the hell is

going on? I go with you to the gym to do legs and I step into an Alfred Hitchcock film."

As soon as we turned the corner, I hailed a cab and suggested that we look at the mysterious object once we were safely ensconced in Michael's apartment.

"Why wait until then?" Michael suggested. "Let's look at it now . . . we're far enough away."

And so we did. I glanced out the back window of the cab to make sure we weren't being followed. We seemed to be safe, so I reached into my gym bag and pulled out the CD-ROM case, my hand trembling as if I held a bloody dagger.

"I don't believe this!" Michael exclaimed. "*ZZ Top— Greatest Hits?!* The steroids that guy is taking didn't just shrink his testicles . . . his brain has lost significant mass, too."

"Now wait a minute, Michael. It doesn't mean that's what's inside. Let's see," I said, prying open the case to reveal just what you'd expect to find in a CD-ROM jewel case: a CD-ROM. But this CD-ROM didn't have a printed label bearing the best of ZZ Top. It was, quite truthfully, blank. "Whatever is on this must be pretty important. Let's go to your apartment and look at it, Michael. We're already downtown."

"Fine, but I tell you, if there's anything on there from ZZ Top, I'll poke my eardrums out."

"I think it's much more than that, Michael. It's so important that the Mafia is after it."

"How do you know those two guys were from the Mafia?" Michael challenged me.

"Look at the way they were dressed. You've seen *The Sopranos*. The Mafia is very hip nowadays."

We were both musing about what the CD contained when the cab pulled up in front of Michael's building.

Michael paid the driver, leaving a tip so small, I ran back to the cab to throw the cabbie another two dollars.

"Why did you do that?" Michael asked. "His cab was filthy!"

"There was one gum wrapper on the floor!" I corrected Michael.

"I call that filthy!" Michael protested. "I've fired house-keepers for less."

Michael was being his old, imperial self. The world, as Michael saw it, was divided into Michael and those who served him. It was as plain as that. Of course, being the heir apparent to a herpes ointment fortune gave him the sort of economic bravado that allowed him to treat sales-people like any of Henry the VIII's wives and waitresses like chattel. This was perhaps why Michael always com-plained that his food tasted like spit when he sent a dish back to the kitchen. His proclamations weren't limited to people who served him, either. He would approach perfect strangers guilty of fashion violations and tell them that what they were wearing was wrong, wrong, wrong. He was like a one-man traveling roadshow of *Queer Eye for the Straight Guy*.

We rode up in the deco elevator to Michael's floor— which he alone occupied. As he opened the door, turned off the burglar alarm that he occasionally activated, and headed toward his computer room, I noticed that the décor had changed again—drastically. This was nothing new since Michael changed his apartment's look the way most people changed underwear (those who bothered to wear it). It had gone from early battleship with rusted steel, raw concrete, visible heating ducts, and bolted I-beams to Italian mini-malist. His penthouse was a sea of excessively calculated nothingness. Two white sofas of impeccable Milan pedigree stood silently contemplating each other. There was nothing else.

"Michael, you didn't tell me that you did your apartment over again."

"Oh yeah, that," he said, barely raising his eyes from his computer screen. "I got tired of the old look. I wanted something cleaner. Ah, here we go," he stated as he inserted the CD into his computer and clicked on the icon. The disk was full of cryptically named folders.

"Click on the one named JRD21303," I suggested. There was no telling what we were about to find. "It looks like a zip code . . . 21303. Where is that?"

The folder opened magically and we were presented with a list of photographs, the .jpg suffix giving away the contents. Michael clicked on one and we found ourselves looking at a photograph of a man dressed in silk boxer trunks wearing boxing gloves and tied up in a chair. I wasn't sure I wanted to get into this.

"I've done that," Michael proclaimed proudly.

I ignored his comment. He clicked on some other folders and the pictures inside. Our next foray brought us face to face with a guy completely encased in an archaic deep-sea-diving suit that looked like something out of a Jules Verne novel. He was suspended in midair by ropes.

"I've done that too. Some guys panic the first time they try it. It takes a little while to get used to," Michael added, pleased that he was in possession of such important, albeit useless information.

"Thanks for the information. I'll remember not to panic the next time I find myself in a deep-sea-diving suit, suspended in someone's living room."

Michael gave me a look of disapproval, then displayed more pictures.

Our next treat was a man dressed in soccer clothing, complete with cleated shoes. Other photographs in the folder showed a distinguished-looking man dressed as a baseball player, football quarterback (I guess), cop, and fireman.

"Boring," Michael commented.

"I beg your pardon, Michael, I have a police uniform. My boyfriend Marc got it for me in Palm Springs, remember?"

"Yes, that was quite an adventure," Michael said with a misty reminiscence.

"We almost got killed . . . several times, and you call it an adventure?"

"Oh, c'mon, it was fun," Michael said, egging me on to agree with him. "Let's go on, more pictures."

It was more of the same. Every kind of kink you could imagine. Guys in rubber . . .

"Done that," Michael commented.

. . . wrestling . . .

"That too."

. . . superheroes . . .

"Been there, done that."

On to other photos. A few clicks and we were looking at a very large baby crawling across a floor—a baby with very hairy legs and a hairy chest.

"I *haven't* done that," Michael added definitively.

"Are you seeing what I'm seeing?" I asked.

"Unfortunately," Michael echoed. "What an ugly baby!"

"Michael, that baby is a grown man."

Michael studied the screen for a while, and like a thousand monkeys typing for millions of years, he actually came up with something—although it wasn't Shakespeare. "Eric is running a sex fetish business and these are his clients!"

I hated to admit it, but Michael had hit the nail on the

head. It wasn't difficult to arrive at that conclusion, but I gave him points for his finding.

"I take it you know a little about this stuff, Michael."

"Doesn't everybody?"

"Most of it's new to me. I mean, I know it exists, but I have no firsthand knowledge."

"Robert, and you whine to me that you can't find a boyfriend!"

"Michael, I'm looking for a boyfriend who won't wet himself at the Union Square Café during lunch."

"You've got to stop being a prude about the Internet, Robert. I get lots of my dates this way. For everyone out there with a special kink, there's someone willing to supply it."

"Apparently . . . and in Eric's case, for a price," I responded, shaking my head in wonderment. "Michael, the names of these folders are probably the initials of the client and the date of their . . . er . . . session. Notice that all the folders end in zero-three or zero-two."

"Look at this one, Michael. I don't get it."

Eric's client was photographed from a very high angle so that the naked client would look very small.

"This guy's into microphilia—or is it macrophilia? He gets off on being made to feel that he's really small."

"You're joking," I replied.

"No, I'm not."

"And I thought my fantasies about gladiators were kinky."

"No, there's a whole group of guys who get off on being overwhelmed by giants."

"Baby Snookums is starting to look better all the time," I said. "Wait a minute . . . Michael, correct me if I'm wrong, but a lot of these guys are prominent New Yorkers."

"Now you're kidding *me*," Michael replied.

"No, I'm not. Open that folder back here." I pointed at the computer screen. "Yeah, that one. The guy wearing the fishnet stockings and bustier is Frank Addams, the fashion designer."

Michael snorted in disgust. "Boy, for a fashion designer, he sure has lousy taste. I wonder why he thinks that bustier goes with those stilettos."

Michael had a point.

"And look," I said, pointing to the initials under the folder when I clicked my way back to it. "FA."

"No!" Michael protested, then looked at some more photos in the folder. "You know, you're right."

"Hey, lookee here, Michael. One of the folders is called *index*." He clicked on the document and before our very eyes were the identities of the men on the CD all neatly laid out for us, in a chart no less. Names, addresses, phone numbers, and sexual fantasies. "Eureka!"

"Boy, Frank is so hot now, I hate to think what these pictures would do to his career if they got into the wrong hands."

"Oh shit!" I exclaimed. "Michael, I think you've just hit on what we've got here! No wonder those goons wanted Eric's gym bag."

"Wow," he replied.

"Oh fuck!" I added.

"What? I suppose now you're going to tell me that the guy dressed in the baby clothes is the model for Baby Watson cheesecakes."

I couldn't tell if Michael was joking or really meant what he just said. Because he wasn't the brightest bulb in the chandelier, there was no way of knowing. It was a good thing he was wealthy and good looking.

"Look here," I said, grabbing the computer's mouse and clicking on a folder. "This guy here is what's-his-name, the Republican candidate running for mayor."

"George Sheffield," Michael said, supplying the answer.

"Right! See, the folder is marked GS. And this folder . . . I've seen that face before. Who is he?" I asked aloud, inviting Michael to help me solve the identity.

"It's hard to tell under the surgical mask he's wearing, but he looks like Allen Firstborn, the televangelist. But I'm sure that's just a coincidence! I can't get a good look at his face because the angle of the photograph and the feet stirrups are in the way."

The folder was labeled AF. Michael was right again, a fact I confirmed after checking some other pictures in the folder. Yup, Allen was getting what some Manhattanites would pass off as a high colonic. To you and I who poop the old-fashioned way, it was an enema. I closed the folder. Ugh.

"So what are we going to do, Michael?"

"What do you mean, what are we going to do?" Michael commented.

"Someone just threw the hottest potato in Manhattan right into our lap . . . and two goons are going to eventually find out we have it."

"No, that's not what I meant," Michael clarified. "I said, 'What do you mean *we?*' I don't remember being a part of this."

It was a maneuver that was typical of Michael. When the going got tough, Michael got going. But I wasn't going to let him get out of this one easily.

"Michael, when those two guys get hold of Eric, they're going to make him tell who has it."

Michael smiled confidently.

"Eric isn't going to tell them a thing, Robert. The guy is

two hundred and fifty pounds of solid muscle and has big tattoos on his biceps. He's not going to talk."

"Michael, just last week, Eric pinched his hand in one of the weight machines and he screamed like a baby. I think we're sunk. I guess we shouldn't go back to the gym for a while."

"Oh great. Can't go the gym?!" Michael stated as if I had just told him that he would never walk again. "Where am I supposed to go?"

"Well," I said, scrambling for an answer, "join another gym for a while. You can afford it. I can't—you paid for my membership to Club M and I can't afford to join another."

"I just can't go to another gym, Robert. This gym and I are in synch with each other."

Then I remembered something. "You're right. You can't go to another gym—you've been thrown out of all the others because they caught you having sex in the shower room."

"Sort of," Michael confessed. "You know how I hate it when you're right, Robert."

"The only course of action is to lay low for now, which, for you, Michael, shouldn't be much of an effort."

"Ha, ha," he replied sarcastically.

"So I'll just leave the CD here . . ." I said, laying the CD case down on Michael's table and preparing to leave.

"Oh no you don't," Michael said, flying into action. He shoved the CD case back into my hand and clamped my fingers down on it with his iron grip.

Oh well, you can't blame a guy for passing the booby prize off on someone else. I snatched the CD and left Michael's apartment. It wasn't just because I was trying to protect Michael that I took the CD home with me. I figured if I was accosted by the two goons in the gym, at least I would have something to give them. Michael could only plead in agony as they put his feet into cement galoshes and dropped him in the East River. On the way home in a cab, I chuckled to myself over and over at the mental picture of the henchmen trying to sink Michael as his pectoral and penile implants kept him bobbing up to the surface. I would have kept on laughing all night long if it weren't for the fact that the next morning, I caught the news and found that Eric Bogert made headlines. It seemed that he, too, had tried to fly off his apartment balcony and forgot to pack a parachute.

2

If Life Hands You a Hot Potato, Make French Fries

The press had a field day with Eric's death. One headline screamed, BODYBUILDER SERIAL KILLER ON THE LOOSE? I tried to ignore the story, except that as I perused the article, there was my name as the proud recipient of the CD-ROM that contained unnamed VIPs in compromising positions. Great. Now the press, lawyers, and assorted psychos had a clear road map to my door. I was a sitting duck.

I sat in stunned silence. How the fuck did the press get hold of that information when I was sure that only the pavement-kissing Eric Bogert, Michael Stark, and I knew who held the dreaded disk? I would never again underestimate the power of the Fourth Estate. For years, I had reveled in celebrity dirt exposed, but now *I* had been exposed and I knew exactly how Jackie O. felt when the press snapped pictures of her changing from a swimsuit into her beach clothes after a swim in the waters off Martha's Vineyard: I felt naked for all the world to see.

In times of crisis, I did what I did best: I panicked. Then I slapped myself and picked up the phone and called Monette O'Reilley, towering lesbian, amateur sleuth, and the person most likely to get me out of this mess.

She answered the phone with a psychic sense of intuition that it would be me. The woman didn't need caller I.D.

"Jeeeeeeesus, Robert! What have you gotten yourself into this time?" she whooped into the phone. "This makes your adventure in Berlin look like child's play."

"Thank you for reminding me that someone just pulled the rug out from under my feet and that my life, dismal though it often seems, is now bleak with a capital B."

"Now, now Robert," she chided me. "There is another way of looking at this matter."

"And what, pray tell, might that be?"

"A lot of people are willing to pay dearly for those photos: the tabloids, corporate competitors, but mostly the guys whose photographs are on the CD you now hold. You're a rich man, Robert."

Monette had a point, bless her. I didn't know the legalities of selling the photographs and figured that blackmail wouldn't be looked upon too favorably by the law, but this was America, goddamnit, and the entrepreneurial spirit that allowed some poor slob like me to make a fortune off the misfortunes of others was a part of what made this nation great. After all, the Vanderbilts and the Rockefellers had built empires off the same principle of taking advantage of a situation and muscling others out of the way with threats and intimidation.

My life was about to become *Gourmet* magazine and *Vanity Fair* all rolled into one. My life would be perfect. I would live in a fabulous downtown loft made of glass and I would wear clothing made entirely of titanium that was comfortable as well as practical. I would listen to jazz and classical masterpieces from microchips inserted into my ears so I wouldn't have to listen to all the stupid shit that people said. I would be driven around Manhattan by my gorgeous bodyguard and sidekick, Ito, in a hydrogen-powered

SUV while I dined on Himalayan Mountain chickens and drank champagne and tossed garbage out the window at the feet of people like Donald Trump. I would—

"Robert, come back to earth," Monette said, breaking in on my pleasant daydream. "I can tell you're tripping off on some fantasy. Hello?"

"I'm here," I sadly admitted, savoring that last bite of grated Gila monster gonads sautéed in sage butter before I came back to reality. "So what's my next step, Monette?"

"Did you make a backup copy of the disk and store it somewhere safe?"

"Yup."

"And the copy is where?"

"On the Internet in my extra-large Yahoo mailbox."

"Good, because you're probably going to have to turn over the original to the police as evidence. You might consider putting the copy in the bank temporarily—in a safe-deposit box. You might consider renting one."

"I already have a box at the bank," I said proudly.

"I'll bet you have all your insurance papers there, a videotape of your possessions, your will, and the U.S. savings bonds your granny gave you when you were three that have grown from twenty-five dollars each to eighty thousand dollars apiece."

"My grandmother didn't give me savings bonds. She was from the Old Country, so she gave me old calendars with the Pope's picture on it. She was afraid to throw them away because they were like holy relics to her, so I ended up with them—like I was going to frame them or something. Just what I wanted on my bedroom walls, Pope Pius grimacing down on me from the year 1957. He still gives me nightmares."

"Are you through?"

"Am I ever?"

"Okay, Robbie my boy, you need to contact the police with your information—if they aren't on their way to you right now. Actually, I'd make another copy of the disk and give the original to the police . . . and handle the real one carefully so you don't smudge the fingerprints on it."

"I think that ship has sailed. Michael was pawing it like Rush Limbaugh after a bottle of painkillers."

"Okay, get off the phone, call the police, and tell me what happened later."

Click. She didn't even wait for me to say goodbye.

I picked up the phone book and looked through the dozens of police phone numbers precinct by precinct. Should I be calling the precinct the gym was in? Or where Eric was murdered? Shit, I forgot how high up on Madison Avenue Eric lived. What if Eric's apartment was in one precinct, but when he hit the pavement, he ended up in another? Or should I call the precinct where *I* live? By the time I figured out the proper precinct to call, I could be murdered.

I picked up the phone and dialed 911. I informed the operator who answered my call for help that this wasn't an emergency *per se*, but it was extremely important. I was bounced from precinct to precinct, from department to department. Then I finally neared my quest. An officer told me to hold the line—he would put me in contact with the detective assigned to the Bogert murder.

The phone was answered by a man with a gravelly voice that had undoubtedly been mellowed and seasoned by years of whiskey and cigarettes. Was I talking to Philip Marlowe? Or was it Sam Spade?

"Detective McMillan here. How can I help you?"

Short, to the point, I thought.

"My name is Robert Wilsop . . ." I began to say, expecting that he would pick up the trail and run with it, telling me that he knew all about me, where I'd been to lately, what clubs I couldn't get into, and how many of my former dates had criminal records. But there was nothing of the sort.

"Yes?" he offered.

"I have the CD-ROM that Eric Bogert gave to me . . . the one with all the photos on it."

"Oh, *that!*" he exclaimed as if he had forgotten something important. "Yes, yes, I would like to meet you ASAP. Can you meet me at the Club M gym in half an hour? I'm doing an investigation there."

Before I left, I made a copy of the original disk and left it on my work desk next to my computer. Then I grabbed my gym bag and workout clothes, and headed down the stairs.

The gym was the last place on earth I wanted to go, especially with a CD-ROM that half of New York wanted to get their hands on, but felt it would probably be safe with policemen everywhere. This erroneous thought was probably the same one that Lee Harvey Oswald had had just moments before he met up with Jack Ruby.

Holding my gym bag tightly, I walked out of my building to take the subway downtown. The moment I stepped out into the street, I knew that my life would never be the same again. I was hit by hundreds of tiny flashes, blinding me. It wasn't a bomb or even a gun—it was much worse. Dozens of members of the press stood outside like a school of starving barracudas. The questions started flying like shrapnel.

"MR. WILSOP, WERE YOU FRIENDS WITH THE MURDERED PERSONAL TRAINERS CODY WALKER OR ERIC BOGERT?"

"DID YOU AT ANY TIME HAVE SEXUAL RELATIONS WITH ANY OF THE TWO MURDERED PERSONAL TRAINERS?"

"MR. WILSOP, MR. WILSOP . . . COULD YOU GIVE US THE NAMES OF ANY OF THE PROMI-NENT NEW YORKERS WHOSE PICTURES ARE ON THE CD YOU HAVE IN YOUR PROSSESSION?"

Now I knew how Princess Diana felt. The reporters rushed me, shoving microphones in my face and clamoring for answers. The only difference between me and the late princess was that I didn't have a single member of the British Secret Service to push the phalanx away from me. One of the reporters actually grabbed my belt and tried to keep me from running away from the questions she peppered me with. I was going to whack her red talon-finger away from me, but I spotted the television cameras capturing my every move, so I thought it best not to strike the bitch down. (My belt-grabbing reporter was clever enough to keep her tether on me hidden from the cameras—she must have been a seasoned pro.)

I felt that I should say something, but every time I saw someone on television utter "No comment," I assumed they were guilty as hell. So I said nothing. I was going to take the subway, but opted for a cab, since I doubted that the wolves would give chase. They didn't. On the ride down, I tried to unruffle my feathers, smoothing my shirt and pants and discovering that when I ran my hand over my ass, my wallet was missing. I decided that the cursed CD was bringing me nothing but bad luck and I wanted nothing more than to ditch the goddamned thing as soon as I could.

When I arrived at the gym, the police were swarming all over the place, going over everything with a fine-tooth comb. I asked several policemen as to the whereabouts of Detective McMillan and was finally told that he hadn't yet arrived. I asked them to inform McMillan that I would be on the treadmill when he showed up.

Not wanting to waste good gym time waiting, I went

into the locker room and changed into my workout clothing, then trotted (healthy people trot) to the treadmill for
some cardiovascular exercise. As I bobbed up and down on
the treadmill trying desperately to drop some extra carbs, I
realized that I was about to tell a New York City detective
that I was turning over the only copy of the CD-ROM
when, in fact, I was keeping the ability to make thousands.
The more I thought about it, the guiltier I felt. I was turning into Barbara Stanwyck and Fred McMurray in *Double
Indemnity*. The guilty can run, but they can't hide, and it
would only be a matter of time before the police surrounded me, ordering me to drop my weapon. I would
burst out of the locker room in a desperate attempt at free-
dom, whereupon I would die in a hail of bullets. The chief
lieutenant, lighting up another Lucky Strike filterless cigarette, would roll my lifeless body over with the toe of his
black-and-white wing-tipped oxford and proclaim that if
only I had given up all copies of the CD sooner, he would
have put in a good word for me so I wouldn't get life in Sing
Sing, playing boy-toy to an inmate named Mugsy.

There was a loud bang and I dropped to the floor faster
than a government informer in Sicily, which wasn't as simple as it may seem. Since I was on a treadmill, I fell on the
moving belt and was ungraciously ejected off to the rear of
the machine with a great series of clattering thumps followed by a skin-burning skid. Ow.

I wasn't shot. Nor was anyone else. The guy next to me
had dropped the book he was reading, and like books have a
tendency to do, it had landed flat as a pancake on the rubber
floor and produced a deafening crack. I looked at the title of
the book: *Wearing Black to the White Party*. I instantly hated
this book and wished ill on its author.

One of the investigators came running up to me, asking
me if I was all right and helping me to my feet. He was

everything I thought a homicide detective should be. His jaw was square and hard—with a five-o'clock shadow thick enough that you could grate parmesan on it. His hair was thick, black, and wavy—the kind you could run your fingers through during a bout of passionate lovemaking. And his eyes . . . they were as blue as Lake Tahoe on a placid day. His olive complexion hinted of Italian-American roots. I could even overlook something that normally bothered me—hairy knuckles. On him, they seemed the very essence of a man engaged in dangerous work. Plus, there was always electrolysis. He was also the right age. I guessed him to be about forty, maybe forty-five. Very sexy, very mature—very tempting. McMillan was not my usual cup of tea, but for some reason I felt very attracted to him. He helped me up.

But I had to resist temptation. I was still in a cross-country relationship with Marc Baldwin, the event planner in Palm Springs with whom I had struck up a relationship after my last visit less than a year ago.

"I'm Detective Luke McMillan, homicide," he said like he was a member of *Dragnet*.

"Robert Wilsop," I said, "clumsy gym member."

Without a moment's hesitation, he began. "Mr. Wilsop . . ."

"Robert, please," I corrected him.

"Robert . . . sorry I didn't connect your name with Eric Bogert's murder right away. So tell me, Robert, how did the press get hold of your name so quickly? Did you call them?"

"No, it was a complete surprise when I saw my name in the story."

"Happens all the time. When I get to a murder scene, the reporters are often there before me. Bad apples," McMillan replied.

"Apples?" I questioned.

"Inside the NYPD. They tip off the press for cash."

"And you think that happened to me?"

"It could have," McMillan said, leaving me feeling rather exposed. The big, bad city really was big and bad. "Did you bring the CD with you?"

"Yes, it's in my gym bag in the locker room. C'mon, I'll give it to you."

I led the way with McMillan looking around the gym as if he had never seen anything like it. When we entered the locker room, he let out a slow whistle.

"This is some place!" he commented in awe.

I had to agree with him. Club M was so nice, you felt bad when you sweated on the floor. The weights were changed regularly when they got bumped or chipped, the machines were so state-of-the-art, I didn't even know what half of them did. And the locker rooms were soft and cushy with deep-pile carpet and subdued lighting and soothing music playing over the hidden speakers. The showers had private stalls with sandblasted glass between them, allowing you to see shapes moving next to you in the nearby shower stall, but not any details. Michael found it sexy while I felt it was expensive and disconcerting—like a peep show where you were the stripper and you couldn't see your audience. But overall, it was a touch of luxury courtesy of Michael Stark and, I guess, Stark Pharmaceuticals.

"I'm going to be so glad to get the thing out of my hand. It reminds me of the Hope Diamond—so much evil attached to it."

McMillan followed me to my locker and I reached up to spin the dial on the combination lock when I noticed that the lock had been cut—someone had gotten there before me.

"Fuck," I said, pointing to the lock that was hanging there pitifully.

McMillan grabbed my hand to keep me from touching the lock further. He took a fountain pen from his shirt pocket and gently lifted the lock from the locker hasp, then pushed open the locker door to reveal my gym bag, its contents spilled out on the floor of the locker. He poked through the contents and surprise—no CD.

I couldn't believe it and I said just as much. "I can't believe it!"

"Someone is really serious about this CD. The place is crawling with the police and they managed to know you were in here, with the CD, and brought a bolt cutter with them."

"Maybe they didn't have to bring the cutter with them," I suggested. "All gyms have metal cutters in case someone loses the key or forgets the combination to their lock. It would've been easy for someone on the staff to know I was here, since they read my membership card with their computer when I came in. They could have easily slipped into the locker room with the cutters, done their job, then made off with the disk." I was proud of my theory and couldn't help feeling triumphant once I heard it with my own ears. I decided to venture further out on a limb. "Since Cody and Eric both trained here, there may be one—or several—accomplices on the staff."

McMillan seemed to mull this over, then took me by the arm, and led me down a hall toward the gym offices. "I need you to come with me where we can talk more in private," McMillan told me.

"Absolutely."

"Good, we'd like to get some statements from you, plus a description of the guys who were following Eric yesterday."

Off we went to the gym office, where he invited an officer with a tape recorder to preserve my observations. I told him about the way Eric was carrying his gym bag closely around the gym, how he became visibly shaken when the two men arrived, and I gave a description of them.

McMillan stopped me to clarify an observation.

"Mr. Wilsop, you described the men who chased Eric as both dressed in black?"

"Yes."

"And you said that they were wearing gym clothes?"

"Not gym clothes," I said. "I know this is going to sound funny, but they looked like they were on a SWAT team or something. They wore cargo pants, black T-shirts, and those police boots . . . the ones made of leather and nylon and the big rubber treads on the bottom . . . for traction."

McMillan cleared his throat. "They're called tactical boots. Mr. Wilsop, how do you know they were police boots?"

"My friend Michael, the one who was with me when Eric gave me the CD, has a lot of police uniforms. So I know."

McMillan looked lost. I didn't blame him.

"Is Michael a policeman?"

"Not exactly. He just likes to wear uniforms . . . on dates."

"I see," McMillan responded. Clearly, he didn't.

"Is there anything else, Detective?" I asked.

"Not right now," he replied. "Here is my card. If you think of anything more about what you saw, call me. Or if you have any trouble, call me anytime day or night on my cell phone."

"Trouble?" I asked. "What trouble?"

"Well, two people have been murdered. We don't know if there's a connection between the two, but Cody and Eric both were personal trainers, both worked at the same gym, and Eric gave you his CD because he wanted to keep it out of the hands of the two guys who were following him."

I felt like the stupidest person on earth. In all the excitement and drama, I never once stopped to think that even though I had given up the CD—or intended to, anyway—it wouldn't matter one iota to the person—or persons—who murdered Cody and Eric. They wouldn't know I attempted to give it up, and it might not matter anyway. Like just about anyone would've done, I looked at the pictures on the CD. And like any even remotely computer-savvy person, I made a copy of the CD. I was in deep shit.

I got up to go, but McMillan stopped me cold.

"One last thing, Mr. Wilsop," McMillan said, firing one more fright-inducing thought across my bow.

"Yes?"

"What floor do you live on?"

The man was trying to see if I were thrown out of my window, would I splatter?

"I'm on the fifth floor," I said.

McMillan stared into the space over my right shoulder and I could see him making mental calculations. Five feet eleven inches, around one hundred and eighty pounds. Five floors, seventy-five feet. Hmm. Head might come off if he hit a fire escape on the way down. No, no, probably would just hit and the organs would come out. Skull would probably show orbital fractures with some brain ejection from occipital region. Well, not as messy as a thirty-second-floor jumper.

Since I had already catastrophized the situation out of reality (a specialty of mine), I at least wanted the validation that I had seen through his glass head. "Why?"

"No, no—nothing. Good locks on your doors?"

"The best. Two vertical deadbolts with pick-resistant locks." I didn't like where this conversation was going.

"Bars on windows?"

"Just on the fire escape windows. Again, the best."

McMillan nodded.

"Am I in real danger?" I asked. I figured if anyone knew about danger, it would be a man who faced it every day.

"No, no. Just keep your doors locked and windows fastened."

"Thanks." I said as I left the office. My fate was clear. I was going to end up in the alley space behind my building with a fractured skull and rats eating my face. A pity, I thought. All those Estée Lauder for Men skin-care products going to waste.

On my way out of the gym, I was going to stop at the front desk to ask if anyone had had a lock cut off their locker lately, when I heard Eric Bogert's name being dropped several times by a bimbo in red workout tights that were—true to their name—tight. Obscenely. The bimbo was conversing with the staff member at the front desk. As I stood patiently waiting my turn, I determined that the Bimbo's name was Adrianne and that she had been Eric's *beau*—her word, not mine. I studied Adrianne's outfit and felt that it was clearly going to waste in a gym that was almost ninety-percent gay, but anyone who dressed like she did obviously didn't get it and wouldn't get it any better if Mr. Blackwell himself stepped into the gym, ripped off her offending garment, slapped her in the face for her sartorial transgression, then entered her as number one on his list of the worst-dressed women.

Adrianne was one of those frightening women that straight bodybuilders seemed to attract. The dyed-blond hair was poofed up and sprayed even though we had entered the twenty-first century years ago, the skin, perma-tanned, and the waist was just big enough to allow her stomach and upper intestines to pass through to her lower extremities. Fingernails were painted an unearthly shade of white—as if she had been clawing at chalky walls with her fingers. You get the idea— not the kind of girl you'd find on an Outward Bound camping expedition. Being a gay man, I had no attraction to this type of woman—or any, for that matter. But I just couldn't

see why men were attracted to these life-size Barbie dolls. I
suppose it was their forced, hyperfemininity. Me, I preferred
tough but sophisticated women like Lauren Bacall, Rita Hay-
worth, and Katharine Hepburn, who were smart, self-assured,
and knew how to make an entrance in a stunning gold lamé
gown at a rooftop nightclub—not someone who was proud
of the fact that she knew the difference between a 1991
Camero and one built in 1992.

"Adrianne?"

"Yeah?"

"I'd like to express my condolences about Eric," I said in
tones that would make an undertaker sound like a cheer-
leader at a UCLA football game.

"Yeah, well, it was so sudden, like."

The babe was from Brooklyn—and apparently, hadn't
ever left it except to come to a gym in New York. I had to
think up some bullshit to keep Adrianne's attention. I though
of swinging a tube of Maybelline lipstick in front of her
face, but decided it would be too rude. It would do the trick,
but it would be rude.

"I just wanted you to know that I always respected his . . .
training abilities . . . with his clients . . . here . . . here in the
gym . . . and he always dressed nice."

"Oh yeah, tanks. I'm shu-wah Eric would've been happy
to heer dat," she managed to get out, then sniffled into a tissue, blowing her nose at the finish like you'd expect a minia-
ture poodle to sneeze: quick and tiny.

"He was always on time, you know—ambitious," I added,
running out of adjectives.

Sniff, sniff.

"Oh yeah, he was ambitious. He had big plans. He was
just about to come into a lot of money from a great awnt,"
she said, giving the word *aunt* such an out-of-place British
accent that I almost started laughing. The Brooklyn re-

turned as quickly as it had gone. You can take the girl out of Brooklyn . . .

"Just about to inherit?" I repeated. "That's so sad."

"Well, I guess I'll get his Hummer. Almost new. A really nice car . . . great sound system . . . sad-e-lite guidance system . . . seats dat adjust a hundred ways . . . not dat any of dat stuff will replace Eric!" she added, remembering that while she would never dress like a grieving widow, she should at least sound like one.

The thought of this bubblehead driving a car of immense weight around the streets of New York and Brooklyn made me shudder. From that moment on, I would walk as far away from the curb as possible.

"Well, I thank you for your time, Adrianne. Again, my condolences."

"Yee-ah, well, tanks," she said, and I left the building.

I had just learned a valuable piece of information: that Cody wasn't the only personal trainer who seemed to be making more money than was possible for a personal trainer to make.

I got on the subway and rode it to work. There, at the entrance to the building where my agency was ensconced on floors fifteen through twenty-three, were the reporters again. Instead of rushing me like they had at my apartment, they stood waiting for me to come into their gaping jaws like a great white shark too lazy to chase its prey. They knew, after all, that I had to enter the building this way and I'd have no other choice but to confront them.

But again, I said nothing. The embarrassing thing wasn't that I was being made to feel like a criminal, but that dozens of my colleagues at work passed by and saw the reporters trying to extract information from me. Clearly, I had something to hide or had murdered someone. I waded through the crowd and entered the building with camera flashes popping from behind the glass lobby doors while I waited for the elevator. And if all this wasn't enough, when the elevator arrived, people feigned excuses for not riding up with me. So up I went alone. Great.

I spent the day writing several ads for a new feminine hygiene napkin that promised thirty percent more absorption. After a day of this kind of thing, it made being thrown out the window of a thirty-second-floor apartment look inviting. But I did it day after day, five days a week, because like ninety-nine percent of the population, I didn't know what else to do—and because I was too afraid to try something else. I was the master of inertia. At five-thirty, my energy returned and I flew out of the building, got on the subway, rode it up to the Ninety-Sixth Street Station, and walked the three blocks home.

When I rounded the corner of my block, they were there again: the reporters. I don't why I hadn't anticipated them being there. Like any normal person, I felt that the Middle Ages were over and you didn't have to live in constant fear of being attacked by anyone who wanted to do so.

I followed my usual routine. I donned my sunglasses, passed through the crowd, and said nothing. I wearily trudged up the four flights to my squalid apartment, put the key in the lock, opened the door, stepped inside, and noticed that there was something different about my place. Instead of being neat and tidy as I had left it, it looked as if Courtney Love had just had sex there. The contents of every drawer, closet, and cardboard box lay strewn on the floor, and every piece of furniture I owned lay on its side with its upholstery slit and the stuffing torn out or the legs broken off.

It's difficult to know what to do at times like this. The average person would walk slowly through the apartment, surveying the aftermath from the depths of a trance-induced stupor. An alternative was to go into hysterics and lean dramatically on walls for balance. Luckily, I kept my head.

I calmly walked back through the door, closed it behind me, and locked it. I made my way down the four flights to the street, where I again dove into the hostile, turbulent waters of the press, made no comment, then walked the three blocks to the nearest pay phone and placed a call to McMillan's cell phone. Luckily, he answered and said to stay outside the building and wait for help, which I did. When the police arrived a few minutes later, the press shifted into a feeding frenzy. The reporters ran for the squad car, demanding answers as to why the police were there. The police calmly ignored them and cordoned off the front of my building with yellow do-not-cross tape. Then, one of the cops yelled my name in an attempt to locate me. I made my way through the crowd, where the police took me inside so they could learn the details of my break-in. I told them about the possible connection to Cody and Eric's murder, gave them the keys to my apartment, and waited patiently for McMillan to arrive. I felt that it would be better if I waited in the hallway of my decrepit building then began wondering if the police might be helping themselves to any of my possessions when McMillan was admitted by a policeman into the hallway. As I was dramatizing my finding upstairs with McMillan, one of the policemen—who had probably stolen my autographed picture of Carl Hardwick, a hunky porno star, given to me by Monette—returned from my apartment and gave his report that the premises had been checked out and the perpetrator was nowhere to be found. This man was a genius. I lived in a studio apartment so small, you had to, as the old joke went, go outside to change your mind. With the exception of my sardine-can bathroom, where you hit the sink vanity with your knees when you sat on the toilet, every nook and cranny was visible from every other part of the apartment—even the roaches had a tough time finding places to hide.

McMillan said he was going to go talk to his buddies upstairs for a few minutes, then would come down and retrieve me when he was sure it was safe. I sat there in the hallway of my crummy building and waited like a good little boy until McMillan reappeared. I climbed the stairs behind McMillan up to my apartment, where I stood there relating exactly what happened when I opened the door. McMillan then conferred with the other two cops about the particulars of the case, and I overheard several facts that seemed mighty peculiar indeed. None of the windows were broken or had been forced open, and the door hadn't been jimmied. I had two deadbolts on my door, both with pick-resistant locks, so entry was unlikely that way. McMillan was about to ask me the next obvious question, whether my landlord had the keys to my apartment, when I cut him short.

"I take pride in considering myself a good and suspicious New Yorker, so after I moved in, I had new locks installed and never gave the landlord or the superintendent the keys. I had a friend who had a fur coat stolen from her apartment and she thinks the super did it, but she can never prove it. My theory was that an enraged member of PETA lived in the building, saw her wearing the fur, broke into her apartment, and stole it. This person was later planning to kidnap my friend, flay her, then sew the coat on *her* back and see how she liked it. But it's just a theory."

McMillan stared at me wordless. "I think we should call an ambulance—you're in shock."

I closed his cell phone for him. "I'm okay, McMillan. My mind always works that way. Frightening, isn't it?"

He ignored my comment . . . or noted it slyly for future reference. "Wilsop, Robert. Burglary victim: definitely crazy. Wise guy, too," was the entry in the notebook of his mind. He shook his head as if trying to dislodge a stubborn thought. "I don't get it. Not a trace of entry anywhere."

McMillan walked over to my only unbarred window. The window was latched, just as I had left it.

"No entry here. It's five stories down, and almost two up if you count the high parapet. Window was latched."

I walked over to the suspect window and had to agree with McMillan: no entry there. The ledge was as clean as a whistle—no footprints, no bits of mortar from a man mountaineering down from the roof on a rope. Nothing.

"Hrrmph," McMillan mumbled, turning his attention back to the front door. He took out a loupe and studied the lock millimeter by millimeter. "Mr. Wilsop, are you sure you locked your door this morning? You're probably under a lot of stress and maybe you closed the door but left it un-locked."

The detective, as much as I was slowly beginning to like him, had just stepped on a land mine and didn't even know it. McMillan had no idea of the extent of my obsessive-compulsive disorder. I checked the locks on my apartment at least a dozen times before leaving for work or before re-tiring for the night. And of course, in checking them, I would also latch and unlatch them to make sure they were truly locked, which made me worry that when I latched the locks, I had perhaps inadvertently unlocked them, leaving me vulnerable and helpless in this cold, concrete jungle we called New York City. I would then open the door and in-spect the locking bolts to see if they were, indeed, being thrown into the door jam, but the very nature of my open-ing the door to my apartment late in the night would com-pletely negate the purpose of the door locks anyway, in which case I would slam the door only to begin the whole purpose of checking the locks again. I won't even go into how often I checked the stove top to see if the gas burners were turned off. Me, crazy? Not a chance. The detective had some nerve.

"So how do you think the burglar got into my place?" I deduced.

"My gut feeling says the front door."

"So you're ruling out the window?"

"It's still latched and doesn't show any signs of forced entry, but I'll go up to the roof to check that out. Is there a door leading up there?"

I leaned out of my apartment door and pointed to the stairway that continued up into the dull, white-blue haze of the buzzing fluorescent lighting that tapered off into darkness.

"I'm going to go up to the roof and check a few things out," McMillan reported. "C'mon, Brady." He motioned to his cohort. "Bring the camera, too."

And up they went. While they climbed the stairs and went onto the roof that I sometimes used for sunbathing, I walked forlornly around my apartment, surveying the disaster at my feet. When I looked at the shambles of my little work desk, I noticed that my Apple laptop was missing. The burglars hadn't bothered to take my ancient TV (not even cable ready), my stereo equipment (which looked like it had been manufactured in the old Soviet Union), or my priceless collection of rusted tractor seats that were mounted on my wall in a display of postindustrial artifacts—an idea that I had seen in an issue of *Metropolitan Home*. I spent a lot of time tracking those seats down in rural Pennsylvania and paying dearly for them. Now I had no idea why.

Twenty minutes later, McMillan and Brady returned. McMillan looked like his foray had answered no questions.

"No success, huh?" I asked.

"Nothing. The edge of the parapet is covered in asphalt

and hot tar—any rope would leave telltale marks. No indication that anyone was lowered on ropes to your window. What I can't figure out is how they got in."

I was no detective, but having been involved in three murders to date, I can safely say that I do have some experience in these matters. And the one question that was in my mind sprang to my lips.

"I think the question is, Detective, why did someone go to so much trouble to get into my apartment in the first place?"

3

My God, Your Apartment Is a Mess!

I was right—terribly right. Someone had gone to a hell of a lot of trouble to break into a fetid apartment just to get their glove-covered hands on the CD that was now in the custody of some unknown person—or persons. The copy that I had made and intended to put in my safe-deposit box was gone—big surprise. I had made the copy and put it in a plastic jewel case and labeled the case (with my label maker, of course—so it would be neat) with the words *Eric Bogert Pictures*. It made it all too easy for the burglar. They had also gotten my laptop computer, but you had to have a password to boot it up, and mine was not your run-of-the-mill password. (I will give you a hint: It's a Lithuanian word for an armless spirit that slams doors and does mischievous things without the use of appendages. Give up?)

Someone, whose pictures were on that CD, would do anything to keep those images from getting out into the hands of the general public, or worse, into the hands of the press. A lot was at stake.

The police finished their investigation, warned me to keep an eye out, and left—that was that. I would have to rely on my own catlike instincts and my trusty mace to protect me.

It was time to swing into action. I got on the phone and called Marc Baldwin, my long-distance lover.

"Hello? Marc?"

"Robert! So good to hear your voice!"

"We just talked yesterday," I commented.

"Yes, but I never tire of the sound of your voice."

Jesus, did I ever strike it rich. I thought they stopped making guys like Marc a long time ago.

Marc continued. "So what's shaking?"

"Me in my boots. Well, my Kenneth Coles."

"Why, what's happening?"

"Someone wants to kill me," I stated blankly. I said it so bluntly, I hardly believed it myself.

"Is Michael making threatening calls to you again for 'stealing his boyfriend'?"

"No, no, he stopped doing that," I answered.

"Oh really?"

"Yes, his psychiatrist doubled his daily dosage of Paxil. He's fine now."

"By the way, how did you know it was Michael calling you? You told me he was using voice-changing electronics."

"He was, but he bought the device when I was with him. Remember, Michael isn't the sharpest knife in the drawer. Plus, he forgets what he's done in the past because he's not interested in anything but himself or what he's doing at the moment. What do you expect from a diagnosed narcissistic, borderline, sociopath personality?"

"Yes, he can be quite a piece of work," Marc admitted.

"Hey, careful there . . . that's my friend you're talking about."

"So what's this about someone wanting to kill you? You're joking, aren't you?"

"No, no I'm not. Technically, they're not trying to kill me yet. But two people who got in the way of a certain someone leaped off high terraces already."

"Got in the way?" Marc asked, the confusion in his mind coming across the phone line loud and clear. "How about starting at the beginning. Tell me everything that's happened."

So I did. When I was finished, there was a long silence on the other end of the line.

"Marc, are you there?" I asked into the ether.

"Yeah, yeah, I'm here. Jesus, it just sounds too unreal. I'm coming out there right away—you need a big, strong man to protect you."

"Marc, you can't leave and come here, especially now. What about the Mercedes launch?"

"It's going to be the best thing I've ever done. Imagine a huge room at the convention center where the walls are undulating panels of stainless steel, the tables are steel, and the ceiling is composed of panels of raw aluminum. Heavy metal."

I was right. Marc, through no choice of his own, ended up rising to the top of one of the largest special event companies in southern California. His latest big project was the launch of the new Mercedes car models for a coalition of southern California car dealers. Germany wanted a big, splashy event and Marc was going to give it to them. He had worked long and hard and invested a lot of his own money to make his special event company one of the best, and I didn't want to stand in the way of his progress.

"Marc, no one's actually *tried* to kill me yet," I stated, talking myself out of impending doom. "The other two guys who did their swan songs from on high were bodybuilders—I am not."

"Robert, no one would ever accuse you of having a huge, muscular body."

"Am I talking with Marc Baldwin or Michael Stark?"

"Sorry, I didn't mean it the way it came out."

"It still sounds like Michael. A backhanded comment, followed by a shallow apology, then a one-eighty-degree change of direction in the conversation about the size of the box on some guy."

"Just kidding, Robert. You have a perfect body, but even better, it's attached to a perfect mind."

I pinched myself just to make sure I wasn't dreaming this guy up.

"Look, Marc, the police are all over this case and they're watching everyone like a hawk. And if they're not keeping an eye on me, the press is taking up the slack. I can't even take a crap without them asking me about it. Just because someone broke into my apartment looking for the CD with all the pictures on it . . ." I began to say.

"They broke into your apartment?!" Marc exclaimed.

"Yeah, but it doesn't mean the bodybuilder killer did it. Eventually, everyone in New York gets their apartment broken into."

"Let me ask you one question, Robert."

"Yes?"

"Did they steal your laptop?"

"Yes."

"Oh, Robert, this is serious. I'm worried for you."

"You ought to be. I had some pictures of me on my computer that I certainly don't want getting out into circulation. I'm kind of wearing a saddle on my back and being ridden by a German count who is naked save some fancy cowboy boots with spurs."

"Robert, you've shocked me! When you were here, I had to plead with you to get you to wear the Desert Storm cammies during sex. I should have tried the saddle first."

The guy had a sense of humor. Monette's wit was razor sharp. Michael . . . well . . . there goes my theory. Since

Michael claimed never to have picked up a book in his life and had little interest in movies or any other form of culture, he had none of the shared-culture base so essential to a sense of humor. Plus, he was incredibly wealthy—or at least his family was. The funniest people, I have found, come from the middle and lower classes—there's so much more to overcome and satirize. From the wealthy person's point of view, there's nothing funny about hearing a story about a debutante playing tennis or a gazillionaire playboy falling off a polo pony. But a middle- or a lower-class person could have you bunching up phlegm over the same incident told from their point of view—on the other side of the polo grounds fence. This may explain why Dina Merrill or Gloria Vanderbilt never did good stand-up comedy.

But I digress.

To sum things up, Marc made me promise to phone him immediately if anything happened and to keep a sharp eye out for anyone suspicious. We exchanged kisses over the telephone, said our goodbyes, and hung up.

I retrieved my protein shake from the refrigerator, drank it all down like a good little boy, then had a quick shower.

While I was sitting on my bed applying moisturizer to my perpetually dry elbows, I dialed a phone number located in Brooklyn. Little did I know that this fateful telephone call would not just change the course of my life forever, but set up a chain of events that would lead to a bloody nose, another body falling from a balcony—this time, in front of my eyes—and a tragic loss to the Leaping Lesbians of Park Slope soccer team.

4

Watch That Last Step—It's a Doozy!

"Hello? Monette?"

"Robert?"

"No, Barbara Eden—who else did you think it was?"

"I saw your debut on the evening news! Are you okay, Robert?"

"Yes, yes, I'm fine, if you don't count my desire to fill one of those oversize squirt guns with urine and soak the reporters that have been dogging me all day long."

"Someone broke into your apartment and ransacked it, didn't they?"

I was stunned. Monette, perhaps the world's greatest unknown detective (and certainly the tallest), was becoming scary in her ability to sense trouble.

"How did you know!" I exclaimed.

"Marc told me a half hour ago."

"So why did he call you?"

"Robert, he's really concerned! This guy's madly in love with you and he asked me to look out for you. So you got broken into, huh?"

"Well, you don't have to sound so calm about it," I remarked.

"My apartment's been broken into dozens of times, but there's nothing to take. After all, who'd steal mystery novels?"

Monette had a point. She claims to have read every detective novel ever written, and a trip to her apartment would confirm that claim. Her modest one-bedroom apartment in the Park Slope section of Brooklyn was lined from floor to ceiling with mystery novels. If you wanted to sit down, you had to move a pile of books. If you wanted to eat something, another pile needed to be shifted. In fact, if you wanted to move in her apartment, you had to step over piles of Dorothy L. Sayers, Sue Grafton, and Agatha Christie. And these were her favorite mysteries that she had kept—she'd donated dump-truck loads of crime novels to the library.

"They get anything?" Monette inquired.

"No, they just wrecked the place searching for the CD, which they got—the copy of it. Oh yeah, they took my laptop."

". . . assuming the CD pictures were on your computer as well. You're lucky someone broke in."

"Why, because it's the first time in years that I managed to get a man in my apartment?"

"No, silly," Monette chided me. "Don't you see?"

"Apparently not."

"Whoever burgled your place thinks they've got the original disk. They might leave you alone now."

"Monette, you're a genius, but you've forgotten one thing: It doesn't guarantee that the murderer got the disk. It could be just one of the guys on it who doesn't want his pictures plastered all over the tabloids."

"True. Are the photos that bad?"

"Well, one of the guys is dressed in diapers and another is having a traffic cone stuck up his bum. You be the judge if you'd want to see that in the newspapers or magazines."

"I've seen worse ones in the *New York Post,*" Monette said. "A traffic cone—that's one I haven't heard."

"You should see the stuff on that disk . . . things I didn't even know existed."

"Like what?" Monette probed.

"Well, I'm not going to go into the disgusting things, but one guy was into being stepped on."

"Kicked?"

"No, stepped on like he was really small, and Cody, the trainer, was really big."

"It's called microphilia," Monette explained.

"How does everyone know so much about this?" I asked.

"The Internet. That, and the fact that I was talking on-line to some lesbian who was thrilled by the fact that I stand six-feet-four-inches tall."

"So she likes tall women?"

"No, it goes much deeper than that. She has a room in her house where everything is really big. You know, chairs seven feet high, dresser drawers so big you have to climb them."

"No, I don't know."

"Guess what her online name was."

"Tiny Tina?"

"Nope. LillyPutian. Get it? Lilliputian."

"Monette, don't you ever accuse me again of making some really wrong picks when it comes to dates. LillyPutian. That puts my feces-throwing Scott in the shade."

"Robert, you make it sound like casual feces tossing. Scott threw his own feces at the mayor's car more than once. He hit Martha Stewart's limo three times."

"Yes, Monette, but at least he was making a political statement."

"A political statement? Robert, need I remind you that he was doing it because the mayor dismissed his plan to dig under Grand Central Station to unearth Hitler's bunker that he claimed was hidden there. And as for the reasons behind creaming Martha Stewart's car, I . . . I . . . think I can muster some sympathy for his feelings."

"Okay, okay, so neither of us have been very successful in the past in securing decent dates," I admitted.

"Well, *you* have. How's Marc?"

"Fine. He's in the middle of some big automobile party. Good money."

"Well, that's nice. Maybe now he can afford to take you in as his boy-toy and you can go live in Palm Springs and swim and write novels all day."

"There's just one little hitch in that plan, Monette."

"What's that?"

"I need to keep someone from murdering me first."

"Now just calm down, Robert. Why don't you tidy up your apartment first, then pack a bag and spend a night over here? And take a cab—I don't want you riding the subway."

"Okay, Monette, but can you keep that Tasmanian devil cat away from me while I'm there? She's always looking at me like she wants to sink her claws into my back."

"Amelia? She wouldn't hurt a fly, Robert."

"The last time I was there, she flew out from behind a cabinet and went for my jugular."

"She was just playing."

"You taught her to hate men."

"Yes, I enrolled her at the Lesbian Separatist Man-Hater Obedience School. Now she only follows the commands of women. I just can't tell which woman—she doesn't do a single thing I tell her to do."

"I'll see you in about two hours. Right now, I have to pick up what's left of the pieces of my life and pack a bag. Lock up the cat, would you—in chains?"

* * *

Park Slope in Brooklyn is only a short cab ride away from Manhattan, but it's worlds away in attitude. Life is slower there, less pretentious, and less competitive. This is perhaps why so many lesbians have chosen to live there instead of on the gilded isle I had just left behind. There might also be something to the fact that while imperious rental agents or real estate brokers might laugh you off the face of Manhattan at the mention of down payments that you thought were enormous, you might actually get in the door of a co-op in Park Slope.

Monette, following this theory, had a one-bedroom apartment that she, unfortunately, didn't own, but rented because the rent was so low. So low, in fact, that she said she would die there and the reality was, rent control had that effect on people's lives: If you got in early, you couldn't give it up. Anyway, her place was on the second floor of a six-story apartment building, but what she lacked in view, she made up for in interior space—all necessary for housing the world's greatest collection of crime novels. It even had a tiny balcony facing the street, reached by a double-hung window that could be thrown open to reveal a space the size of your average bath mat that was actually the roof for a bay window for the apartment downstairs, but Monette's entrepreneuring landlords had seized on this opportunity like a fly on the proverbial pile of shit and had a small platform built to enable a person foolish enough to stand on it to do so. Anyway, the balcony, which was now home to a huge pot of white geraniums, beckoned to me as I arrived in front of Monette's building. If you had cataracts, blocked out the occasional honking car horn, and had three zombie cocktails in you, you'd swear you were in Tuscany. *Bellissimo!*

Monette buzzed me into the building and I climbed the

stairs to the second floor, where my Amazon friend with the flaming red hair stood waiting for me like a old friend—which she was.

"Robert, c'mon in," she bellowed, clapping me on the back like a longshoreman with an anger management problem.

It was just Monette. Being six foot four inches and of ample frame, it was easy for her to underestimate her own strength. But there were compensating factors. She was the star player for her champion lesbian soccer team, the Leaping Lesbians of Park Slope. With a clear shot, she could kick a field goal from more than halfway across the field, taking out the goalie in the process.

I looked everywhere for her hellcat, Amelia, but she was nowhere to be seen. I spotted Monette's bedroom door down the hall and noted that it was closed, and hopefully the she-lion was on the other side of it, bolted in.

"Just put your bags anywhere, Robert. You know, I was thinking about your *situation* for a while."

I am about to be murdered and she's calling it a *situation*. I wondered what she called a mass murder?

Monette moved a pile of books the size of the Boulder Dam and sat down in a purple upholstered chair. "I don't think anyone wants to kill you—at least not yet."

"Gee, I feel better already, Monette."

"No, now listen up and stop trying to be funny—which I know you are." She gave me a little wink that made me feel that everything was going to be fine. "If someone wanted you dead, they would have done it already. They got into your apartment. They could have been waiting there, hiding in your bathroom with a garrote in their hands. You walk in, and screech!" she said, throwing an imaginary rope around my neck and tightening it with a quick pull of the arms. "It's quick, easy, and best of all, quiet."

I sat there, too terrified to move—or breathe. I could feel the rope around my pretty little neck already, the gloved hands of my assailant briskly rubbing against my ears as I struggled to stomp on his foot and free myself. He would go down like dead weight as I would spin around, whisking the Walther PPK from my concealed suit jacket holster and firing several times into the body of my assassin. I would adjust my bow tie, brush the dust off my tuxedo, and seat myself back at the baccarat table. Bond. James Bond.

I heard Monette's voice from afar.

"Robert? Tell me something. You didn't see the news broadcast of you coming out of your building this morning, did you?"

My reply was instant and decisive. "No, and I never want to see another news program again as long as I live, which is saying a lot since I love Katie Couric."

"Well, I think you should see what I recorded while I was at work," Monette gently suggested. "I don't normally record the news, but with the circumstances you find yourself in, I wanted to keep an eye on how the media is handling you."

"Why, I didn't say anything to the reporters. You didn't happen to catch any of the reporters lifting my wallet from my back pants pocket, did you?"

"No, but I got something you should see and I want you to sit down when you watch it."

This wasn't looking good. I could tell Monette was handling this issue with the delicacy of a bomb diffuser with Parkinson's disease. *Careful* was the word.

She moved a pile of books on the sofa along with a catnip toy and put them both on the floor at my feet. She slipped a videocassette into the VCR and there I was leaving my building, gym bag in hand. I watched as I stood on the top step, confronted for the first time by the reporters and the flashes of their cameras and the spotlights of the television cameras. I watched myself stand there, my genitals showing from the gap in my pants fly, which I had forgotten to zip up.

"OH MY GOD. OH MY GOD. OH MY GOD!" I exclaimed in agony.

"That's exactly what I said when I saw it."

"OH NO, I CAN'T BELIEVE IT!" I screamed again, shaking my head in agony and covering my eyes, hoping that this was all a dream. I uncovered my eyes for an instant and discovered that it wasn't.

"I can never go out in public again!" I lamented. "The one day I don't wear underwear because every pair is in the dirty clothes pile and I haven't been to the Laundromat is the one day I walk out in front of dozens of reporters with my fly open."

Monette had a smile on her face and was desperately trying to suppress it. "Maybe we should change the subject for now. You said that whoever broke into your apartment took your laptop?"

"Yes, but it was insured. At least one thing is going my way—if you can look at a burglary as a positive event. Now I can get a bigger model."

"I'm so happy for you. Anyway, can they open your files, or are they protected in some way, like with a password?"

"Both. Just to log into my computer, you need to have a password. Then the file is protected too. But you'd have to be a genius to figure out the password."

"Is it *berunkis?*" Monette suggested.

"How the fuck did you know? No one knows that word, except for my grandmother, Martha the Obscure."

"Oh, c'mon, Robert. You use that word all the time. You think it's safe because no one knows Lithuanian. You made the fatal mistake of telling me one time—I just figured that you would use it because it was as obscure as the tales your grandmother told you."

"Anyway, the only way to get the computer usable again is to erase the entire disk and reformat it, destroying the contents at the same time."

"Okay, so whoever stole your computer knows that it's inaccessible but they have your laptop and the CD that was lying next to it on your desk. So they probably think their work is done. We might be able to eliminate one culprit from our list of suspects."

"Yes, but who? We haven't even started asking them questions," I reminded her.

"It's better than nothing. The one suspect that seems the least interested in getting their hands on the CD might be our murderer."

"But what if my burglars aren't the actual murderers— just men who want to keep their secret sex life just that—secret?"

"That's what we're going to find out over the course of the next few days," Monette responded. The girl already had a plan. "We say we've still got the CD, or a copy of it, and we use that as our leverage to get in to see our suspects."

"Yeah, and look where it got the first person who tried that: on Madison Avenue, being scraped off the pavement with putty knives."

Monette held her arm high into the sky as if waving to a bird of prey. When Monette was on to something, she could get pretty dramatic with her hands. Thank goodness she didn't have priceless Ming china in the house.

"In all this confusion, we need to stick to the basics. First, who would resent having to pay blackmail money for the pictures? And second, who had the opportunity to commit the crime? What was the name of the first guy. Uh, Obie . . . ?"

"Cody. Cody Walker," I corrected her.

"Yes. So he had this sideline business . . . making people's fantasies come true. So why kill the second bodybuilder? What was his name?"

"Eric Bogert," I answered.

"Yes, Eric. I would think that killing off the first personal trainer would be enough to scare the second into abandoning his blackmailing. See, we don't know enough about what happened before the two murders. If we understood that, we'd know the motivations the killers have. Robert, I think it's time we got on the Internet. I may be a committed lesbian, but I'm dying to see what a traffic cone looks like up a man's butt."

5

How the Hell Did That Get Up There?

We gathered around Monette's computer in her living room and watched eagerly as the screen came to life.

"Now where did you store the pictures?" she asked, clicking her way around from site to site. I gave her the website address where I have online storage facilities. She clicked on the folder marked *Vacation Pictures* and downloaded the contents to her own computer.

"Hey, those are *my* pictures," I said as I now realized that myself and a very clever burglar were no longer the only owners of the incriminating pictures.

"I can't believe you, Robert. Here I am assuming great risk to myself by downloading these potentially valuable pictures and you're being stingy. Plus, this way, I can look at them at my leisure without having to go on the Internet."

I looked at her skeptically.

Monette rolled her eyes back at me in response. "Robert, I know that my sex life isn't that good right now—okay, ever—but sitting around with a vibrator inside of me looking at pictures of naked men . . ." she said as she clicked on one of the folders and was presented with a man doing, well, what I thought was impossible. ". . . successfully sitting on a mature eggplant is one of the last things I can imagine doing. Look at it, Robert, he's swallowed the—!"

"Yes, I see . . . the whole vegetable! Monette, dear, could you please click on another folder . . . this is something I don't want to see."

"Okay, let's go about this thing logically," Monette suggested. "I think we're looking for two different people. One stole the original CD from your locker. The other, from your apartment. I can't believe the two are the same. What I'm theorizing is that our suspects are so desperate to keep their pictures out of the public eye, that everyone is about to go over the edge—and two just did."

"Yes, Monette, but stealing a compact disk and murdering two people are not quite the same thing."

"True, but I said some people are quite desperate. They killed to suppress the CD, then broke into your locker and your apartment to get the disk."

"So now that they think they have the disk, they might rest, right?" I said hopefully.

"Let's hope so," Monette replied. "Okay, it's time to make a list of our suspects so we can go strong-arm them into giving us some information."

"Monette, these guys aren't going to let us blackmail them into telling us information."

"Remember, Robert, if you're going to be a great detective, never assume."

"Because you make an *ass* out of *u* and *me*," I added, reciting what hundreds of college kids before me have heard by nerdy professors thinking this was the first time their class ever heard it.

"Okay, let's go through the index of Eric's clients, match them up to their particular fantasies, and come up with a list of suspects."

Click, click, click. Monette moved from the index to the

various client picture folders. "Check *this* out," she implored me.

I peered into the computer glow to see a man with a heavy five-o'clock shadow with barrettes in his hair and heavily applied lipstick dressed in a bustier with hot pants and hairy legs tucked into red-hot marabou mules. It was like watching an extremely bad drag show.

"Now I know where Frank got the inspiration for his last collection," I said.

"Frank Addams. Forced feminization." Click, click. "Add that to the pad, Robert," Monette instructed me.

"Check," I replied.

"Chet Ponyweather. Horse-riding gear, ass beating with a riding crop. Wears a horse saddle occasionally. Hey—you and Chet have something in common, but his top rides sidesaddle—very proper."

"Very funny. Got it. Proceed."

"George Sheffield, Republican mayoral candidate, into dressing like a baby. Now where the hell do you get oversize infant clothing like that?" Monette asked to the air around her.

"Baby Gap for Big and Tall Men?" I offered.

"Two points, Robert."

"Uh-huh. Next."

"Oh fuck me backwards on a tractor!" she blurted out in tones that would not only wake the dead, but make them put their boney hands to their ears. "Hardcourt, my boss! He's into wearing superhero outfits!" she laughed. "I don't believe my luck today. Spiderman, Batman, and here he is tied up as Robin. Heh, heh, heh, something tells me I'm going to be getting that raise after all. Are you getting this down, Robert?"

"Yes, Hardcourt, Robin, Spiderman . . ."

"And the saddest-looking Batman I've ever seen. Not

even Adam West on TV's *Batman* was that paunchy. It's a good thing he's wearing that chest plate with the built-in abs. Okay, okay, I'll stop. On to the next."

Click, click.

Monette began shouting in horror. "Please, gouge out my eyes! I've seen the flabby ass and Baptist-sausage-and-pancake-church-supper stomach of televangelist Allen Firstborn!"

When she was done performing her theatrics, her eyes lit up and sparkled like supernovas. "Allen Firstborn . . . ALLEN FIRSTBORN! I DON'T BELIEVE IT! It's like someone just gave me a banana cream pie and a clear shot at Dr. Laura!"

It was too good to be true, but there he was in the flesh, literally.

"Eeeeeuuuuuw!" the two of us chorused.

Monette shielded her eyes in horror. "I don't ever want to see anything like that again. Oh, are we going to have fun with this!" Monette squealed, which was quite something since Monette was not the kind of woman who squealed.

"You read my thoughts exactly. And Monette . . ." I said, placing my hand on hers in mock seriousness. "No matter what happens to me, you get these pictures to any Rupert Murdoch newspaper, okay? Promise me."

"You have my solemn word, Robert. So was Allen doing what I thought he was doing before I considered gouging out my eyes with grapefruit spoons?"

"If you lived on upper Park Avenue, you'd say he was getting a high colonic."

"Very tastefully presented, Robert."

"Thank you."

"I assume that there is some kind of fetish thing going on here. You don't think he's one of those overpampered people who can no longer take a dump like normal people?" Monette asked.

"I think this guy is into medical scenes. See the speculum on the rolling medical table?"

"Bravo, Robert. A good point well spotted. You know what I'm noticing about all these photographs?"

"That it makes you want to swear off sex completely?"

"That too. No, none of these pictures have Eric in them. Cody seems to have taken them all. I'm getting the feeling that Cody did all the work and Eric did the blackmailing."

"I've had the same sneaking suspicion," I added.

We continued to go through the folders of clients, with me making detailed notes on our legal pad matrix. Monette looked at me with a sudden seriousness. "Jesus, now I know just how badly people want to get their hands on this CD. Millions of dollars are at stake here . . . in political circles, religious circles—and we've just begun to lift the rocks up in this messy affair. There's no telling what will crawl out next."

Without taking my eyes off the computer screen, I asked, "Monette, you're not sorry you let me stay here for the night, are you?"

Her reply was instantaneous. "Heavens no, Robert. We've been through three murder cases, wars, famines, and one showing of *Dogma*, with Ben Affleck and Matt Damon. No, I wouldn't desert you in this time of need." Just to emphasize the point, she gave me one of her rib-cracking hugs. "You did take more than one cab, didn't you?"

"To lose the reporters?"

"Well, them, but, more importantly, someone nastier."

"Oh, Mr. X? Yes, I took several. I even had cab number two do an illegal U-turn on East Seventy-Ninth Street, followed by a dash down Eightieth, then back onto the FDR Drive."

"Good boy. Okay, first things first. We need to know who's after that CD because until we do, your life isn't worth a plugged nickel."

"Well, when you put it like that, Monette, my future all seems so bright."

"You know what I mean. Now who is the detective assigned to your case?"

"McMillan. Luke McMillan."

"Yes, Detective McMillan. Unfortunately, he is not going to come out and give you a lot of information because that's privileged for the grand jury. But I think we have enough to go on with our little fetish matrix. Don't you worry—we'll find out who's after you—and why.

"Wow, I just can't get over how rich Cody's clientele was. It looks like he did most of his calls to the clients' apartments. Jesus! Look at these apartments, Robert! The guy in the last folder had a place on Fifth Avenue, around Eighty-Fourth Street, judging from the position of the Metropolitan Museum in the photo. Outrageously expensive furniture, stunning views. Look at this guy's place, Robert. A genuine Van Gogh on the wall."

"Wow. How can you be sure it's Van Gogh?"

"It's early Van Gogh. Look at the brushstrokes. It's his usual theme, too. Peasants in rural France. Coming out of a church on a Sunday morning in autumn. Beautiful."

"Do you think it's real?"

"Without a doubt. Rich people don't have posters and framed copies from the Metropolitan Museum gift shop on their occasional tables. No wonder someone's going to such extremes to get that CD. There are reputations at stake. Some of these guys could be the CEOs of companies that manufacture household cleaners that Methodists in Kansas use to clean their toilets. Knowing that the CEO likes paying a personal trainer to stick fruit and vegetables up his bum isn't going to fly very well with its customers, whose brains have been disintegrated by these very cleaning products. No, these people will be out for blood. The guys on this disk are probably shittin' on their priceless Persian rugs right now."

"Did you notice the Picasso etching on the table in that one guy's apartment . . . the one wearing the riding outfit in the last folder?"

"Chet Ponyweather's? Yes, I did notice it. I also noticed that Frank Addams has several Julian Schnabels in his apartment."

"Hmm, there's a lot to be explored here," Monette remarked, closing folders and putting her computer to sleep. "Well, I think that's enough for tonight. How about bad movie night?"

"*The Testicles from Planet Eros?*" I asked.

"Robert, forget about exposing yourself for the cameras. By tomorrow, everyone will have forgotten about it. How about *The Beast with a Million Eyes*? And I could make my famous nosebleed nachos . . ." Monette suggested like a sadistic Julia Child.

"How about a pizza?" I countered.

"Robert, you always love my five-alarm nachos."

"Of course I do, but not tonight. My stomach's upset about this mess I'm in."

Grabbing my chin, Monette looked straight into my eyes, and perhaps into my heart. "Remember, you're not in this thing alone. I'm always here."

"Thanks, Monette. You're the kind of friend I need right now." I was silent for a moment, then changed the subject. "Besides, I need a pizza because I'm not getting any younger, Monette. The last batch of your nachos taught me the meaning of the word *flaming asshole*."

Monette gave a loud laugh that stopped short of cracking

plaster. "Okay, I'll call in the pizza. But at least let me have some jalapeños on it."

"On *half* . . . I want mushrooms on my side."

Monette opened a bottle of red wine, popped the tape into the VCR, and we waited for the pizza to arrive. Monette didn't start the movie just yet—that would be blasphemy to watch a bad movie without a slice of cheese pie in one hand and a glass of wine in the other. So we talked about nothing important for some time until the door intercom blared in Monette's hallway.

"Yes?"

"Pizza delivery," the voice yelled.

(Why, I wondered, do people always feel they have to yell into the intercom? If you would just talk in a calm rational voice, you'd be heard loud and clear. But no, everyone has to talk so loudly, they make the entire point of the intercom unnecessary or cause so much distortion that you can't hear the person on the other end.)

A minute later, there was a knock on the door. Monette opened it.

"Mmmm, smells wonderful!" she said. "So where's Gino?" Monette asked.

"Gino?" the deliveryman asked.

"Gino, the usual delivery man."

"Oh, he sick," pizza man replied.

"Well, tell him I hope he feels better."

"Okay, I'll tell him," the man said, smiled, then closed the door gently behind him.

"Movie time," Monette announced, carrying the pizza box into the living area, where we sat on the sofa she once rescued from a dumpster and watched the movie to its pathetic conclusion. True to my fear, my nose started bleeding after eating one too many jalapeños.

When we had finished the movie and cleaned up,

Monette helped me prepare the sofa in the living room for my slumber. As I climbed into bed, I asked the question that had been on both of our minds since before I arrived.

"Monette?"

"Yes, little Jimmy?" she said like a mother with 2.3 children living in Cleveland, Ohio.

"Monette, I've been here a whole evening and you haven't played one practical joke on me yet. In fact, I've been waiting for the other shoe to drop after the last one I played on you."

"I assume you're referring to the incident where you sent that e-mail to me at work labeled *Compromising Photos of Ellen DeGeneres*, and when I opened it, the damn thing shot the volume control on my computer way up and screamed, 'Hey, everyone! I'm looking at porn over here!' Everyone on my floor heard the fuckin' thing."

"Yes, I recall that I might have had some kind of remote connection to that occurrence."

"Robert, it had your signature style written all over it," Monette said, giving me a sly look. Don't worry, you'll get yours," she added with an evil grin.

Ever since I met Monette over a decade ago, we both enjoyed playing practical jokes on each other. I think it was the soul mate connection we had with each other that made us both enjoy it, and it was the mental combat that kept things exciting.

I bid Monette good night and settled down to a well-deserved sleep. The noise from the street kept waking me up since I was used to sleeping in a room in the back of a building. It's funny how living in New York can make you appreciate the difference between sound levels that would deafen those used to the quiet of the suburbs. My apartment on the Yupper East Side was like sleeping inside the muffler of a taxi cab, and Monette's apartment was like the inside of a Pratt & Whitney jet engine—it was a difference that mattered.

At around two-thirty, I awoke to faint noises coming from the window facing Monette's balcony. Again, I'd slept right through several fire engines a few blocks away, but awoke because of some tiny scratching noises.

I got up, rubbed my eyes, and went over to the window only to find a man wearing a ski mask partially protruding through an opened window a mere twelve inches from me. The man stared at me for a second and I stared at him, neither of us moving a muscle. Suddenly, there was a horrific, primal growl behind me as I turned to see two glowing eyes racing toward me from Monette's bedroom down the hall. Amelia must have chewed through her chains, pried opened the bedroom door with her meat hooks and was now barreling down the hall toward my face for a taste of blood. Fifteen-pound Ameila bounded through the air and hit me like a linebacker for the Dallas Cowboys, causing me to lose my balance in the darkness and fall back against the window and our burglar. The window, which our nocturnal guest had apparently propped open, came down on his head like a guillotine blade with a sickening bang. Dazed and contused, Mr. Ski Mask raised the window enough to extract his aching head backward, letting the window slam shut a second time. Ameila had landed on the ground nearby and crouched there, growling at me with eyes afire while the burglar (or was he an assailant?) stood unsteadily outside on the balcony, trying, no doubt, to figure out what had just happened. While he was regaining his composure, I went into action.

I grabbed the nearest heavy object and tossed it through the window at the burglar. The burglar, startled not only by my appearance but also by an unknown object crashing through a window, fell backward over the edge and disappeared, followed by Monette's 2002 Big Apple Lesbian Soccer Championship trophy.

Monette flew into the living room like a bat out of hell (which was what she resembled until she had her first cup of coffee in the morning), asking, "What the hell is going on here?"

"Someone just tried to break in here, and I threw something at him," I shouted.

We pushed back what was left of the window and stepped out onto the broken glass of the balcony in our slippers, figuring that we'd be looking down onto the crumpled corpse of the burglar, speared perhaps by Monette's trophy in a twist of irony—but what we saw was even more amazing. The assailant rose from the sidewalk below and sprinted off, then hobbled, followed by more sprinting, then more hobbling in a painful dance of escape.

We both sat looking down at Monette's trophy, lying sadly—but intact—below on the street. During its trip down with our burglar, it must have bounced off the convertible roof of a car parked at the curb and landed somewhat safely in the street.

"Thank Goddess that you and the trophy are safe," Monette said with obvious relief.

Just as Monette's uttered those words, a taxi came barreling down the street and clobbered the trophy with a speed that left us with jaws agape. The moment of triumph of the Leaping Lesbians of Park Slope was no more.

"Well, one out of two ain't bad," Monette commented.

6

The Law of Falling Bodies

We spent the rest of the night talking to the police, including Detective McMillan, who was very understanding for two-thirty in the morning.

We told the police and the forensic technicians everything—so much so, that by the time the majority of them had left, the sun was coming up. I decided that I might as well go back to my apartment, shower, shave, and go to the gym. I know, I know, you would think that the last place I would be seen was in the gym, but I had worked my tail off to get my body lean and mean for my boyfriend, and no ski-masked bandit was going to stand in my way of that.

McMillan suggested that I be driven back to my apartment by one of the policemen standing in the hallway, where I would be escorted up to my place and seen in the door safely. I didn't have much to say to the policeman who drove me home, but I couldn't help think that if Michael had been in my place, he would've been raging with lust right now. Michael had a thing for men in uniforms—especially police, military, and firemen, in that order.

I was seen up to my door by the policeman through a crowd of reporters that had, amazingly, started to dwindle somewhat. I turned the key in the lock and was about to dismiss my protector when I realized that my apartment had been broken into again. All my tidying up had been a waste of time.

More cops again—and Detective McMillan. More of the same. More questions, more racking my brain trying to remember "anything that might help." More shit.

I showered and dressed for work. When I got to my office (a windowless telephone switching/computer server room), I launched into the first order of the day: begging Michael for a place to stay until this whole thing blew over.

I dialed Michael's private number. (He had one number for his intimate friends, one for tricks, and one for the rest of the world.)

"Yes?" came the sleepy answer.

"Michael?" I asked because I wasn't sure.

"Robert?"

"Michael, it's ten o'clock! What are you still doing in bed, you whore?"

"I was up all night . . . I was staying up with a sick friend."

I felt guilty right away.

"Michael, I'm sorry about the joke. Is your friend all right?"

"Oh, he's fine. In fact, I just sent him home."

"Michael, do you think that's wise? I mean, maybe he shouldn't be outside."

"Robert, what the hell are you talking about?"

"Your sick friend."

"Dearest Robert, I said he was sick."

"Yes, well . . . ?"

"I said he's *sick*. He likes to make love through a piece of uncooked liver, then fry it and eat it."

"Michael, why do you do this with him?"

"Because he's hot. But I have to put a stop to it."

"Because it's unsanitary?"

"No, I hate liver, Robert. It's a filter organ."

"Michael, I have something to ask you."

"You want to borrow my pair of Frank Addams leather shorts?"

"No. I need a place to stay until this is all over."

There was a long, pregnant silence on the other end of the line.

"Oh, Robert, you know how I would *love* for you to stay with me, but I'm full up here."

"Michael, you have dozens of rooms in your penthouse."

"Yes, but most of them are full of my hobbies."

"You can't have all of your rooms filled with welding equipment. Michael, tell me what this is all about. I would let you stay in my apartment as long as you had to."

"Yes, Robert, but I wouldn't want to stay in your apartment."

"No, there's some reason you're not telling me why you don't want me there."

"Well . . ." Michael hesitated. "For one, it would cramp my style."

"You mean you would feel funny dragging home a trick in front of me?" I suggested.

"Exactly," Michael replied with a sigh of relief.

"Michael, you have never let me stand between you and a hot date. Remember that time you had sex with that military guy while I was still in the cab? You didn't even wait to drop me off at my apartment."

Even over the phone line, I could tell Michael was staring dreamily off into space.

"Yes, he was good, wasn't he? And that high-and-tight haircut! Let it never be said that I don't support our troops!"

"Michael, the point is why you don't want me to stay at your apartment."

"Oh, *that*. I don't want you to bring me any more bad luck."

"Bring *more* bad luck? What have you done now?" I asked, knowing full well that Michael had done something very illegal or highly offensive.

"You know those fuckin' rocks I brought back from Maui?"

"The ones you said would look good on your terrace garden? You didn't tell me they were from . . . oh no . . . Michael, you didn't desecrate some ancient Hawaiian burial ground, did you?"

"Not exactly."

"What did you do?"

"The Hawaiians believe that spirits inhabit the rocks, and if you remove them from the islands, the spirits inside get angry and fuck up your life until you return them."

"And how, pray tell, did they screw up your life, Michael?"

"The day after I got back from Maui, I was dancing at the Metal Club and my leather pants got torn on a loose nail. The next morning, I spilled coffee on myself at Starbucks. See?"

I failed to see the connection between ancient Hawaiian spirits and tearing pants at an attitude-filled dance club, but I let Michael continue or there would be no end to it. Michael, more than anything, loved to talk about himself and, even better, to draw people into his misery, no matter how trivial.

"I know you don't believe that this is all connected because you're not *spiritual* like me. I won't even bother to tell you about the person who stole my cab from me."

Michael had a point there. In my memory, no one had

ever stolen a cab from Michael and gotten away with it. I knew this for a fact since I'd witnessed an incident one Christmas season. Michael and I were shopping in the Village and we decided to take a cab to Soho for lunch. Some princess in a fur coat and expensive boots ran out and grabbed a taxi that was clearly ours. Michael confronted her, heated words were exchanged, and Michael put an end to the stalemate by dragging the girl from the cab and throwing the princess into a pile of slush at the curb, coat and all. His pièce de résistance was to throw her shopping bags into the slush with her. He pulled me into the cab and off we sped with the tempestuous tulip shouting obscenities at us until we were out of earshot. Merry Christmas!

"Well, Michael, just get rid of the stones and their bad luck," I suggested. It was too simple of a solution, however.

"You can't just throw them out!" Michael retorted. "You have to have someone of true Hawaiian ancestry take them back to Hawaii and restore the spirits to their resting places."

"And how much did this set you back?"

"What makes you think money was involved?" Michael asked.

"With you, there always is."

Michael hesitated, then volunteered the information. To most people, what he was about to tell me would make him look just plain foolish, but to Michael, he confessed because it made it clear that he had big sums of money to throw around.

"Eight thousand dollars."

"EIGHT THOUSAND DOLLARS!" I almost screamed. "Let me guess, you had some guy in Hawaii offer to take the rocks back to Hawaii first class, then there was a fee for interring the rocks back to their proper settings."

"You're forgetting the hotel bill here in New York. He

had to stay here for five days to draw up maps to determine from where I had taken the rocks."

"And that cost eight thousand dollars?"

"Well, the guy had to eat while he was here. You know how hard it is to find good Hawaiian fusion cooking here in Manhattan?"

"Let me make another guess, Michael. He just had to go to Paia, the most expensive and overrated fusion restaurant in town?"

"Well, I couldn't send him to Food Emporium to pick up a can of pineapple and some mahi mahi."

Sensing that Michael's mind was possessed by Kalikakala, the goddess of stupidity, I played the only trump card I had left to play: I reminded Michael that I had once saved his life from a group of fag bashers. That seemed to do the trick. If there's one thing that appeals to a narcissist like Michael, it's the fact that you prolonged his life so that the rest of the world could be eternally grateful that they merely existed. What can I say? I was desperate.

I called Monette and told her to meet me at the Oyster Bar at Grand Central Station, a convenient meeting spot because it was roughly halfway between her office and mine. I said it was time to start interviewing suspects.

"Well, who do we start off with?" Monette said as I handed her the list of suspects.

"Monette?"

"Yes, Robert?"

"Are you sure this is such a good idea, questioning these guys at work and at home? What if they go after us with a knife or a gun?"

"Calm down, Robert! We're holding the trump card here. We have the pictures. These guys will behave themselves because they don't know what we might do with the pictures if they threaten us. Plus, I have another idea concerning the CD. It's not just enough that we ask some questions. We need to lure the real killer into the open."

"And how do you propose to do this? Handcuff me to a chair in my apartment and leave the door open for the killer to finish me off?"

"Close. No, while we're questioning these guys, we drop the fact that we have the CD safely in your apartment." Monette smiled demonically, pleased at something so simple and yet so clever.

"So that someone desperate enough to kill two personal trainers will break into my apartment and retrieve the CD? Of course, we know that the police are watching the apartment and they'll be caught?"

"You forgot the most important part: without putting your safety in jeopardy."

My eyes lit up like Times Square on New Year's Eve.

"I like it, I like it!"

"Good."

"So when are we going to visit these guys? I have a full-time job . . . and so do you," I reminded her.

"We do it on our lunch hour just like we're doing now. Most of these guys have their work phone on this list. We just call them, say we'd like to discuss the pictures, and we see where it goes."

"Okay, why don't you come over tonight and we'll do this—at Michael's apartment. I'm staying there until things cool down a little. I should be safe in his penthouse, unless someone has the ability to climb up the wall like a spider."

"Good idea, Robert, although with some of the trash Michael brings home, you might be safer off elsewhere."

"Like where?" I asked.

"In prison."

7

Nice Kayak You Have There!

I had slipped home through the reporters, who hounded me with questions as to where I was going, gathered up enough clothes for a few days, and headed downtown to Michael's place, taking three cabs in order to shake any reporters who might be following. Monette arrived at Michael's place at seven.

"He redecorated again?" Monette asked as I let her into the apartment.

"Two months ago."

"So what do you call this look?"

"I think its post-communist-Metropolis-deco-minimalist."

Michael changed the look of his apartment for three reasons: One, he could afford to. Two, he got bored easily. And three, he was afflicted by the one disease suffered by so many New Yorkers: chronic trendiness. These people had one motto and lived by it no matter how foolishly they dressed, how much they spent to stay current, and how long they waited in line at the restaurant *de jour*: Amaze me or I will dismiss you.

I led Monette down the hall to the smallest room in his penthouse, which Michael had begrudgingly turned over to me. Michael's welding torches and acetylene tanks sat un-used in a room next door, paneled in stainless steel and equipped with a king-sized bed. But no matter: My tiny room was a safe place to sleep.

Monette threw her backpack on the floor and followed me down the hall to Michael's computer room. Monette gasped when I pushed back the sandblasted glass door to the room and revealed Michael's latest makeover.

"My Goddess! It looks like a NATO control room buried under a mountain in Colorado. I can't believe this!"

Monette wasn't exaggerating. The room was nothing short of incredible. There was a stainless steel console table facing a huge plasma TV screen, which Michael had gotten rigged up to his computer. There was no looking at a tiny twelve-inch computer screen for Michael. No, you cruised the Internet on a forty-seven-inch screen TV with a sound system that probably rivaled Steven Spielberg's private home movie theater.

"Is this all for the computer?" Monette asked in wonder.

"No, Michael has all his audiovisual equipment here too. He has a rack of twenty CD players that play music twenty-four hours a day. You don't hear it now because he has it turned off. But when it's on, you just have to walk into a room and a motion sensor detects you entering then switches on the music for that room. It's all-trance, all-the-time."

"Jesus," Monette replied. "And I thought when I got my latest Apple computer, I was on the cutting edge."

"Well, at least you have a computer. Mine is sitting in the hands of some murderer."

Monette was still looking around the room in amaze-ment when she seemed transfixed by something.

"Robert?"

"Yes. Monette?"

"Why are you and I looking up at ourselves on the TV screen?"

"Oh that! Michael has several webcams focused on various parts of the room."

"For chatting, I suppose," Monette said skeptically.

"That's what he calls it. *Chatting*," I said, putting vicious quotation marks around the word *chatting* with my fingers. "I call it lining up sex partners on the Internet."

"And having online sex, too."

"I'm sure of it," I replied, clickety-clacking my way on the Internet.

Monette slowly rose from her leather console chair and inspected the seat for signs of, well, unpleasant stuff.

"Ah, here we go," I said as I downloaded the pictures onto Michael's computer. We had no sooner opened the first set of pictures on the screen than we both looked at each other and laughed. We had to—there wasn't any other choice. When you stepped back and looked at the situation, it was like life: Truth was stranger than fiction. The best writer in the world couldn't make this stuff up.

"Oh, I almost forgot," I interjected. "Eric Bogert, the second trainer to play high-altitude leap frog, was planning on coming into a lot of money soon."

"Never assume," Monette reminded me.

"Yeah, but what do you think, Monette? I mean, the guy has a perfect piece of blackmail in his hands and, at the same time, tells his girlfriend that he has a rich aunt who's going to die to cover his newfound money—not to mention drives a new Hummer."

"It looks pretty incriminating to me," she said, clicking on photographs. "I wonder why personal trainers have this *in* to people's lives?" Monette pondered.

"The reason is simple, Monette. Personal trainers, after all, are like hairdressers: People tell them everything about their personal lives. The trainer, if he's got anything on the ball, just sits back and waits for the right moment to pounce. You've got Mr. Uptight Wasp on Fifth Avenue, doing dead lifts with Cody or Eric, casually mentions that he was watching *The Horse Whisperer* the other night on DVD, and before you know it, Cody has the guy bent over a saddle with his riding pants down around his ankles and is swatting his butt with a riding crop. You don't have to give these clients a very big push because they want it so bad."

"That happens with my hairdresser all the time," Monette replied. "He's working a machete through my hair and boom—I'm dressed in a French maid's outfit asking him to paddle me with the backside of a hairbrush."

"Uh-huh," I said. "I think licking honey off Ellen DeGeneres's breasts while she sits on the back of a Harley-Davidson motorcycle is more your style."

"You have no idea of what I'd do," Monette replied. "Well, actually, I have no idea either—it's been a *long* time since I had sex."

Just then, a voice coming from behind us scared the bejesus out of Monette and me. "I'd go out of my fucking mind!"

"Michael!" I exclaimed, the adrenaline still pumping through my bloodstream.

"Hi, Michael," Monette echoed.

"So what are you two up to?" Michael asked.

He sat in a chair and listened as we told him about our intentions to question the various suspects, starting with John Bekkman tomorrow at lunch. When we were done, he sat still as if drinking all the information in.

"You know, something like this happened with me a few years back. This guy was following me around town. It was fall, because I remember he wore a trench coat and a hat with a wide brim that almost hid his face in shadow."

Suddenly, both Monette and I were intrigued.

"Well," Michael continued breathlessly, "I leave Barney's, walk a few blocks, and notice that he's still following me. So I dash down this alley trying to lose him, only to find out it was a dead end."

"Holy shit!" Monette exclaimed. Even she was on the edge of her chair. "So how did you get out of there?"

"I didn't. He comes down the alley after me and I get into a corner and crouch down."

"And?" I demanded.

"He walks slowly toward me, grinning this evil, sadistic grin. He opens his trench coat and pulls out a gun with a silencer the size of a rolling pin and aims the gun at me and pulls the trigger."

Monette, always interested in crime stories, volunteered the likely outcome. "The gun doesn't fire and you run out of there like a scared rabbit?"

"No, we made love then and there, on the garbage cans."

Michael had done it again.

"Michael, are you sure he didn't pistol-whip you, because you're talking like a person who suffered a serious head injury," I offered.

"No, no, he was a guy I was dating and he told me he'd always wanted to play a hit man. So we worked out this fantasy of his ahead of time, he was the hit man and I was the innocent, vulnerable victim. It was scary and hot at the same time!"

"Michael, how is being stalked and almost assassinated hot?"

"It's all that power! Plus, it's the thrill of playing someone you don't get to be in normal, everyday life. That's the fantasy. Who wants to have vanilla sex all the time, the same ol' in-and-out all the time?"

Both Monette and I raised our hands.

"See, that's why you two haven't had sex in so long. You're too limited."

Thinking that he had taught us a valuable lesson, Michael got up from the chair and left the room.

"You know, Monette, I see his point. If I had just let that guy with the ski mask attack me at your place, I could've had the greatest orgasm of my life."

The rest of the night was fairly uneventful. There were no goons chasing me, no masked assailants lurking at windows, and no ransacked apartments to clean up. I puzzled over this whole affair that I was involved in. Life is like a huge wave sometimes. You see it coming, but you stand on the beach frozen in fear, knowing that you're going to get hit and carried wherever the wave wants to take you—there's nothing you can do about it but wait until the wave has lost its power, then swim back to shore. Fighting it won't do any good—it will just tire you out. And as I remember my father saying to me as I waded into the ocean for the first time when I was nine, "The best swimmers are always the ones to drown." Thanks, Dad. To this very day, I won't go very far into the ocean.

The next morning, Monette and I had our list, ready to contact our first blackmailee at lunch: John Bekkman.

I did a little research on John Bekkman and what I came up with was fascinating. He was the quintessential renaissance man. He did what he wanted when he wanted. While that may at first sound like Michael Stark, they were worlds apart. You would never catch Michael kayaking on the East River at five-thirty in the morning. Michael wouldn't dare to backpack across the Himalayas, let alone fly over them. ("Nothing to do there!" I could hear Michael saying.) And you would never see Michael giving away several grand masterworks of art to the Metropolitan Museum—or giving anything away, except for the occasional dose of crabs.

John Bekkman was the man I wanted to be. Correction, the man I was *supposed* to be. I always felt that I was switched at birth and was actually born to a wealthy family that spent its time reading obscure books in equally obscure languages, traveling to exotic countries that were barely on the map, and engaging in sports that had changed little since the ninth century. But some lunkhead nurse returned me to the wrong crib in the hospital nursery and I was taken home by a hopelessly middle-class family to a middle-class city and lived a middle-class life. And here I was, in John Bekkman's apartment on Fifth Avenue, staring right in the face of what I could have been. I could have had sandy blond hair (okay, I could still dye it from my teddy bear brown), an athletic body that looked like it was always thin, wear simple but chic clothing, wear driving moccasins with no socks, and live on Fifth Avenue with a knockout view of Central Park and be surrounded by an impeccable collection of art. It was like Steve McQueen had come to life as the character of Thomas Crown in my all-time favorite movie, *The Thomas Crown Affair*. I doubted that John Bekkman was a high-caliber bank robbery mastermind like Thomas Crown was, but you had to wonder where his money came from. Was it possible to inherit *this* much money? Monette, never one to be impressed by signs of wealth, was clearly wowed and she said so.

"Nice place you have here," she commented.

"Thank you, Ms. O'Reilley."

"Yes, in fact, I don't think I've ever seen such a personal collection like this before," Monette gushed again. "I'll bet that when you have too much art, you rotate them around just to keep things interesting."

"Something like that," Bekkman answered coyly.

"I just mentioned that because I noticed that you changed the color of your walls since you had Cody Walker in here for your sexual fantasies," Monette stated cheerfully.

I watched John's reaction and thought I detected a minuscule shudder run through his body, but it was hard to tell. He was so cool about it, so in control, that I wasn't sure. Of course, being hit with an ice breaker like Monette's reference to his sexual fantasies could rattle just about anyone.

"I change the wall colors because I rotate my paintings in and out of storage. I can't put my Kandinsky on the same pastel wall where my Cassatt just hung. That's why the wall is red now."

Monette pushed on. "Yes, well, lovely. Could we ask a few questions about Cody Walker and Eric Bogert?"

John folded his hands and shifted himself into a more comfortable sitting position. He seemed to expect that we were going to read him a story.

"Ask all the questions you want," was his reply.

"How did you first develop your *relationship* with Cody Walker?" Monette queried.

"*Relationship?* Cody was just a sex partner, Ms. O'Reilley. I met him through the gym."

"Is this Club M?" she pried further.

"Yes."

I chimed in. "I'm a member, but I don't remember seeing your face there."

"I dropped my membership there a long time ago, but I kept my sexual rendezvous with Cody for some time . . . that is, until his partner, Eric, approached me and tried to extort money out of me."

"Did he succeed, Mr. Bekkman?" Monette asked.

"Yes, yes he did—to the tune of fifty thousand dollars."

I almost choked on my own saliva. Even Monette was surprised.

"Wow," Monette commented once she had digested Bekkman's response. "No wonder Eric had a expensive car."

"And what kind of car did Eric buy with my money?"

"From what I hear, a Hummer."

"Good car," Bekkman responded.

Monette raised her eyebrows.

"Oh, so you have one too?"

"I've had one since long before they were popular. I use it to get me to places where an ordinary four-wheel drive won't take me."

"I see," Monette said. "Mr. Bekkman, can I ask you why you paid the money to Eric when you seem to be independently wealthy? I mean, you have no employer or a business of your own to worry about being tinged by scandal."

"True, but I have something you can't put a price tag on: my image. I am known the world over as an adventurer, and outdoorsman extraordinaire. That image means more to me than any amount of money, which I have plenty of. Notoriety is the only currency that means anything to me."

Monette nodded as if John's answers made perfect sense—and to me, it did too. There are some things in this world more important than money. Offhand, though, there wasn't anything I could think of at that moment.

"So you had these fantasy scenes with Cody, but Eric was the one who asked you for money to prevent the release of the pictures?"

"Yes,"

"Did Cody know about this blackmail arrangement?"

"I don't know. I stopped seeing him after Eric demanded the money."

"Interesting," Monette said. "Mr. Bekkman . . . John, where were you on the nights when Cody and Eric were killed?"

"I told Detective McMillan already. I was in the Sierras backpacking with three of my buddies . . . days away from any town. He checked out my alibi and gave me the green light."

Monette turned to me and asked me if I had any questions. I nodded my head. Just one, I remarked.

"Mr. Bekkman, are you single?"

My question provoked a great, riotous laugh, not at me, but at the question. It was funny seeing Bekkman laugh so hard when normally he seemed to be in control of his emotions. Not repressed, but in control. There was a profound difference. I guess you had to keep a level head when you faced the things John did: bears, crocodiles, raging rapids, blinding snowstorms, and the odd glacier.

John looked me straight in the eye and returned my serve. "Are you, Mr. Wilsop?"

"Semiattached."

"Like a garage, huh?"

I liked this guy's sense of humor. Of course, I had no sooner said what I did than I got hit by a thunderbolt of guilt. I felt that I had betrayed Marc all the way back to Palm Springs.

"I guess that's all, Mr. Bekkman," Monette finished.

As John was showing us out of the apartment, he said one last thing.

"I guess that money I paid to Eric was all for naught. Now you have the pictures. I suppose I have to pay you next?"

Monette turned to him and said, "As long as you give us the answers we're looking for, the pictures will remain with us safely at Robert's apartment. No charge."

"Thanks," Bekkman replied.

Bekkman smiled and closed the door gently behind us.

As we were waiting for the elevator, I spilled my guts to Monette.

"Why do I feel so sorry for a guy who's got more money than anyone could possibly use?"

"Strange . . . I feel the same way, probably because he was the victim of an unscrupulous blackmailer. It doesn't matter that he has scads of money, because money doesn't seem to mean much to him. He's afraid of losing a reputation that means a lot to him. He's right, you can't put a price tag on that."

"Speaking of price tags, did you see the view from his apartment?"

"Right over the Metropolitan Museum and into the park."

"Monette, I'd kill for a view like that."

"Perhaps you're not the only person who thinks so, Robert."

8

Riding Miss Daisy

The next day at lunch, we pounced on Chet Ponyweather, a man with an address on upper Madison Avenue and an affinity for wearing a fox-hunting getup and having a riding crop used on his bare posterior. Getting in to see Chet at his office in Midtown was easy. I merely told his secretary that I wished to discuss the matter of his personal trainer and some portraits I had done of him in his apartment. The secretary, clueless as to what was really going on, commented how nice it was to see Mr. Ponyweather finally getting some portraits of himself done so that *his wife and children could enjoy them*. How much goes on right under our noses without us ever realizing what's happening?

Monette and I were ushered into his office, which was decorated, naturally, in high-WASP. It looked more like a gentlemen's club than an office. From what I could tell, the firm that Chet apparently headed had something to do with shipping.

Chet had all the markings of a bona fide WASP. The wiry red-blondish hair was combed to the right (never the *left*, mind you) with generous dabs of some hair mousse designed so that heterosexual men could look presentable without appearing too gay—the perfect cover for the closeted husband. The two blue eyes that sat deep down in his windblown face like pools of stagnant water at the bottom of a very wrinkled well said it all. They suggested years and years of exposure to the elements—on sailing boats, watching polo matches, and gardening with his wife on the extensive grounds of their country home in Litchfield, Connecticut. Everything about Chet seemed tightly controlled. From the gold, signature cufflinks (probably from Brooks Brothers) to the starched white shirts and the shoes that were probably polished daily (including the bottom soles—I noticed as he sat across from us), Chet was a man whose life was circumscribed by generations of rigid social structure and manners that promised severe punishment if broken. No wonder Chet liked to get his butt beat—it was just a sadistic metaphor of his everyday life. But despite the thick, insurmountable walls that separated Chet from the unanointed, unprivileged masses yearning to get inside, you could sense it wouldn't take much to make those walls come a-tumblin' down. The profuse sweat that appeared out of nowhere on Chet's regal forehead and on either side of his WASPy, upturned, and diminutive nose said that this was one scared rabbit.

"So," Chet started off, "you said on the phone that you have some pictures of me?"

"Yes," Monette answered. "Taken by Cody, your personal trainer."

"Cody Walker? Good God," Chet sputtered. "Messy business, that."

(The guy even talked in a syntax that no one spoke anymore.)

"Yes, we just wanted to ask you a few questions, Mr. Ponyweather," Monette stated.

Chet looked like he was about to burst into tears at any moment, had it not been for the fact that a man in his social position couldn't cry, especially in front of proletarians like Monette and me.

"Okay, okay, Mr. Wilsop and Miss O'Reilley, how much do you want for the pictures?"

Monette shot me a glance that, no matter how fleeting it was, told volumes. It said, "This could be it, our ticket to early retirement, the end of money worries, substandard apartments, and the beginning of long, Caribbean vacations." At the same time, however, it also said, "We can't—it wouldn't be right. It's not a moral issue, really. It's more the fear of getting caught."

Fortunately or not, reason—and fear of jail time—prevailed.

I spoke up, ending the uncomfortable silence. "Mr. Ponyweather, we're not here to blackmail you by asking for money. We're here to ask you some questions."

"Are you with the police?" he asked.

"No, but we are involved in this matter—and we do have possession of the CD with the pictures of you on it. Robert has them safely stored at his apartment."

"So you're *associated* with Eric, are you?"

His inflection on the word *associated* made even me feel slimy.

"No, no we're not," I answered.

"Then why aren't you trying to blackmail me like Eric?"

Monette's face lit up like the Christmas tree at Rockefeller Center. "Eric was blackmailing you?"

"Yes," he replied in low voice designed not to carry any farther than our ears.

"Mr. Ponyweather, we know you're a member of Club M. When did you begin training with Mr. Bogert?"

Chet looked perplexed. "I've never trained with Eric. My personal trainer was Cody Walker."

Confirmations for our theory about Eric doing the blackmailing and Cody unaware of it were flying left and right. Monette spoke first.

"You made these pictures with Cody, correct?"

"That's correct," Chet said promptly.

"So how did Eric get his hands on them?"

Chet blew his nose, stifling back a sudden case of the sniffles. "That, Miss O'Reilley, is something that I'd like to know. I suppose that Cody was working with Eric in this messy business."

It was my turn to ask a question. "Mr. Ponyweather, did Cody ever approach you asking for money in exchange for the pictures he had taken of you?"

"No, just Eric."

Chet sat quietly in his chair, the leather squeaking occasionally as Chet shifted his weight ever so slightly. What struck me about Chet at this point was no matter how comfortable his surroundings seemed (and believe me, they did look comfortable—even sumptuous), Chet never seemed to be at ease. This state, I felt, wasn't brought about by the recent events facing Chet. I think his whole life was uncomfortable, ill at ease. Having been raised Catholic, I knew intimately how he felt.

Chet took a different tack. "So you say you have possession of these pictures?"

"Yes, yes we do," Monette answered for the both of us.

"For the love of God, please don't release those pictures—it will ruin me, my marriage, my family."

"We're holding on to them for now, Mr. Ponyweather," Monette said, carefully choosing her words. She didn't want to give too much away right now. "I need to ask two more questions."

"Go ahead, you hold all the cards," Chet conceded.

"How did Eric let you know he wanted money in exchange for the pictures of you and Cody?"

"Why, my dear, he came up to me in the locker room and just plain told me."

"He never sent you a letter?"

"No letter. Just brazenly walked right up to me and told me. Oh, he did give me a manila envelope and told me to open it."

"And what was in the envelope?" Monette queried further.

"A picture of me and Cody, printed out on paper. He said he wanted there to be no mistake that he had all the pictures of the two of us. 'Just an example of what I got on you,' he said. And your second question?"

"Where were you on the night of Cody's murder and Eric's?"

"When Cody was killed, I was having dinner with a business partner at the Four Seasons. The night of Eric's murder, I went out for a walk."

"A walk?" I asked.

"Yes, unfortunately."

"Unfortunately?" I inquired.

"Yes, not the kind of thing that gives you a perfect alibi, considering that Eric's apartment was only a few blocks from mine."

"Interesting," was Monette's only comment. "Mr. Ponyweather, I think those are all the questions we have right now. Thank you for your time."

I got up and followed Monette out of the office and into the reception area. The receptionist smiled grandly at the two of us.

"I hope that you capture the true spirit of Mr. Pony-weather in your portrait!" she gushed as if her life revolved around her restrained boss, which it probably did.

"I think someone else already *beat* us to it," Monette told the perky woman—the double entendre sailing clear over her head.

9

I'll Fight You for That Dress

Day three of our lunchtime interviews took Monette and I to the epicenter of the fashion world: Seventh Avenue. Next on our list was one of the hottest fashion designers around: Frank Addams. In true designer fashion, Frank had been working for years relatively unknown, turning out tight-fitting, colorful, unisex Lycra jumpsuits that were probably snapped up by people far too out of shape to wear them. Then, 9-11 happened, followed by the invasions of Afghanistan and Iraq. Frank, seeing a golden opportunity, jumped on the militarization of the United States and began turning out military-inspired clothing in bright colors. His brilliant marketing ploy, coupled with the hiring of a hot publicist, made Frank an instant success. The fashion press—as usual—screamed in headline type sizes usually reserved for World Wars that Frank's embrace of all things military would change the way men and women dressed in the twenty-first century. Instead of merely going to work or dinner, people would storm offices and restaurants with fashion bravura, decimating hostile bosses and haughty hostesses in a victory guaranteed by leather cargo pants, Desert Storm cammies in silk, and Ultrasuede flak jackets. As usual, the call of the fashionistas went unheeded by the masses, but Frank had managed to tap into the deep-seated feeling of insecurity and helplessness that characterized the trendy and monetarily foolish strata of society and they began paying huge sums just to be the first on the block with a real Frank Addams. No, Frank had his finger on the pulse (or was it the jugular?) of America. It would, however, be a cold day in hell before we would be seeing Baptist housewives in Dallas, Texas, donning Frank's creations to wear to the local Piggley Wiggley for groceries. But no matter how you looked at it, Frank was as hot as hot can be.

His offices said that he was hot, too. Some equally crazed interior designer had spent a lot of money to make the lobby look like Baghdad the day after it was invaded by U.S. troops. Large, simulated blast holes penetrated several walls, permitting visitors to get a glimpse of Frank's *troops* furiously working to rush fresh supplies of his bellicose collection to stores everywhere. Equally disturbing was the fact that mannequins were poised climbing through the holes, raising defiant fists and dirty rifles and garbed in the latest Addams, conveying the unmistakable message that Frank wished to telegraph: Frank Addams is victorious in the war of designers.

"Will you look at that?" I said, gesturing toward a mannequin that had apparently jumped through a plate-glass window in Frank's lobby, her acid green paratrooper jump suit giving her all the protection she needed to leap unharmed through glass shards and smite the cunt-of-a-saleswoman at Bergdorf Goodman who looked at her sideways. "I'm afraid that all this belligerent fashion is going to lead to scores of people going postal. It's like a license to kill. I mean, people are so angry already nowadays."

"No doubt. Soon the news will be filled with stories about fashion rage," Monette replied.

"You know, if Frank's girly pictures get out, can you imagine what they could do to his image?"

"Now, Robert, are you hinting about the macho image he tries to convey on television?"

"Yes—quite over the top."

"You mean like Ralph Lauren's carefully cultivated image that he's some kind of old-line WASP?" Monette replied.

"Yes, like that."

"Oh! Listen to this, Robert!"

"What?"

"You know when we had the pizza delivered to my apartment a few days ago?"

"Don't tell me it was poisoned," I relented, figuring that life couldn't get any worse.

"No, it's better than that! Remember when I was surprised that Gino, the guy who regularly delivers the pizza, was replaced by another deliveryman?"

"Yes."

"Well, it turns out I saw Gino delivering pizza last night in my neighborhood and I told him I hoped he was feeling better."

"So?"

"Robert, Gino said he wasn't sick. He told me some guy approached him and told him he was a good friend of mine and that he was going out for cigarettes. The guy said he was heading back to my apartment and would take the pizza back for Gino."

"And I suppose that the next thing you're going to tell me is that you think the mystery pizza deliveryman and our burglar/assassin were one and the same?"

"You betcha," Monette said, nodding her head in affirmation of my conclusion.

"Okay, so the reason he came to the door was to case the

joint for points of entry and gauge the resistance any occupants might offer," I reasoned further.

"Probably. If he'd meant to attack us there, he would've done so. But there are two of us and only one of him."

"And thank God I had the lesbian equivalent of Mike Tyson with me," I joked.

Monette looked me straight in the eyes. "You know I'll get you for that, Robert."

"I have no doubt about that, my little Belle of Ireland," I said, patting her on the shoulder.

Presently, a fashion victim posing as a secretary met us in the reception area and ushered us to Frank Addams's office. Frank was seated behind a cobalt blue desk that was stacked high with fashion drawings, model headshots, and fabric samples. The walls were painted a bright orange with framed black-and-white photos of soldiers from World War II. The ceiling was a sunny yellow. Even Frank's eyeglasses were tinted a deep red. There was no doubt about it—Frank's father must have been Benjamin Moore. I looked down at my black pleated trousers, black shoes, and black T-shirt. I felt like a black hole.

Frank shuffled through stacks of papers, talking to us as if we were hidden in the papers he riffled through. "SowhatcanIhelpyouwith?" he asked, firing words at us like a machine gun with a jammed trigger.

Monette cleared her throat and began. "Mr. Addams, we just want to ask a few questions about the murders of Cody Williams and Eric Bogert."

Frank continued shuffling and talking at the papers. "Inmyopinionallbodybuildersandpersonaltrainersandpeoplewiththinmuscularbodiesshouldbemurdered."

I could see both Monette and myself shoot a glance down at our toned bodies, wondering if we were going to be stabbed at any moment.

"Idon'tknowifIwanttotalkaboutanyofthis."

Just then, there was a knock on the door and a woman with a figure that wasn't made for Frank's clothing entered with an envelope.

"Francis," the woman pleaded, "Marakova backed out for the show. She said—and I quote—that 'zhe von't vear das ug-lee clothes dat da fuckhead Frahnk Addumz dezines. He insult me lahst time I vuz here for his assho fashion show ven he say Marakova need to vehr the deodorent cuz she smell like de Russian army."

Frank put his head in his hands.

"Did you say that, Frank?"

"Eileenyou'veknownmeforyears—youknowIdid," Frank admitted.

"Frank, I warned you to take a few Zolofts before the show," Eileen reminded him. "You know how you can get a little wound up and you tend to fly off the handle."

Eileen was being kind. Frank was like a badger on speed.

"Frank," Eileen continued, "now the public relations department will be giving me shit because they'll have to do damage control so the fashion press doesn't get ahold of this. You know the trouble we had when the press found out your garments were being made in China by slave labor."

"Eileenthereyougoexaggeratingagain," Frank protested. "Theywerecriminalsworkingofftheirsentencesforreading bannedbooksbyDanielleSteel."

Eileen huffed at Frank. "Some of them were shot when they didn't sew their daily quota of capri pants."

"CanIhelpthat?"Frank exclaimed. "Youcan'tdoanythingin thiscountryanymorewithoutsomeoneboycottingyou!PETA hatesmeforshowingfurlastyear.Lesbianshatemebecause thetunaservedatmyStopWorldHungercharitydinnerwasn't dolphinsafeandtheNationalOrganizationofWomenhatesme becausemymodelslookedliketheyhadbeenbatteredwith clubs. OkayEileenwhatdoIhavetodotogethertoforgiveme?"

"She says you have to . . . to . . . stick your head . . . uh . . ." Eileen stalled, searching for a way to express what the three of us in the room already knew.

"ThatwillbeallEileeenthankyou.Iwillcallherlaterandthink ofsomething."

Eileen left the room as exasperated as when she'd come in. I found myself fascinated by all the idiocy of the goings-on, but lunchtime was ticking away and we had gotten nowhere. Monette tried to get things moving again.

"Frank, could we get down to the bottom of things?" she asked.

"Ithoughtwehad," Frank stated.

"No, the only thing that was discussed here was that you would not stick your head up somewhere that would be physically impossible. My partner here and I want to ask a few questions."

"Fineifitwillgetthetwoofyououtofhere."

Monette began. "So which personal trainer did you have at Club M?"

"Personaltrainer?!" Franksnorted. "Honeydoyouthinka manwithafigurelikethisevergoestoagym?Incaseyoudidn't noticeI'mfatfatfatfatfatfat!"

"So how did you meet Eric or Cody?"

"Idon'tknowanEric.JustaCody."

"But if you didn't belong to Club M, how did you meet Cody?"

"Oneoftheguyswhoworksformehererecommended him.HebelongstoClubM."

"Could we talk to this person?" Monette asked matter-of-factly.

"Noyoumaynot."

I tried a different tack.

"Frank, did Cody Walker talk to you about paying money in exchange for the pictures of you?"

"No,someotherguy.Bigguy."

"Was his name Eric Bogert?" I hinted.

"Eric?" Frank said. "EricEricEric.Yes,thatwashisname. Nevermethimbeforethetimeheaskedformoney.Ifiguredhe wasworkingwithCody."

"That's something we're not sure about," I answered. "Did you pay Eric for the pictures?"

"Why?!"

Frank didn't seem to care about anything except dealing with a furious runway model who was probably shooting up as we spoke.

Monette tried one last question.

"Frank, you haven't tried to retrieve these pictures, have you?"

"Retrievethem?Whatdoyoumeanretrievethem?" Frank spat.

"Robert has the pictures on a CD in his apartment for safekeeping. You know, you wouldn't break into someone's apartment and take them back?"

Frank twisted his face in horror. "Breakintosomeone's apartment?HoneyIcan'tevengetintomy*own*apartmentwith outthesuperhelpingme.Enoughquestions!Ihavetogettowork socouldyouleaveme?"

Monette and I got up, shrugged our shoulders at each other, then left the office wondering what the hell we had accomplished. Monette was looking particularly defeated.

"I fucked up," she confessed.

"We did not, Monette."

"Yes, I did. I had no line of questions prepared. I didn't ask the right questions to test my theory."

"What is your theory?"

"I don't know. I thought Frank would give me an idea for one."

"Monette, we're just trying things out."

"Well, I think we can safely assume that Eric got hold of the CD without Cody knowing about it and decided to blackmail Cody's clients. In three out of three stories so far, Eric is the one who approached the clients. Cody doesn't seem involved, except for the hustling part and the staged sex scenes. Cody probably got pushed off his terrace without knowing what Eric had done, then Eric was forced to do his own swan dive."

"I have to agree with you, Monette."

She scratched her flaming red mane. "I feel there's more to come. What I don't understand is why, if you want to get your hands on the CD, would you kill Cody or Eric? It's like killing the goose that lays the golden eggs."

"Maybe our Mr. X was pissed . . . pissed at Eric trying to extort money from him, whether he got the dough or not."

"I don't know. Revenge on top of retrieving the CD? That is weird, but maybe," Monette commented. "Maybe if you can't get to the CD, or you're not sure if there's a copy, you just kill the holder and hope that the CD and any copies get misplaced by a relative who inherits the possessions and throws the CDs away thinking Cody or Eric was into kinky sex."

"It seems like a stretch, Monette."

"You're right, Robert. The killings don't make sense— right now. That's what's bugging me. This is so different from many mysteries. See, we already know who the suspects are. We even know their most likely motives—to prevent a scandal. I just feel that we blew an opportunity to get some real answers. We've got to remember that we're not just out to solve these murders. The main thing is that we figure out if someone is really after you, if they're capable of causing you serious danger, and who is behind it all."

"You don't have to remind me, Monette. That fact is very much on my mind right now."

As we stood on the corner of Thirty-Eighth Street and Seventh Avenue, a blue van came screaming out of nowhere and headed right toward us. Like a movie in slow motion, we watched the van jump the curb with its two right wheels and come scraping the sidewalk with its axles in a shower of sparks and screeching metal. It was the worst thing you could imagine. Well, not as horrible as watching the *Anna Nicole Show*, but it wasn't pretty.

Monette, whose quick reactions made her the star player on her lesbian soccer team, pushed me back behind a light pole into relative safety as the van came slicing along the sidewalk, missed the pole by a good six feet, crashed back into the side street, and fishtailed back and forth until it was out of sight.

Monette came running toward me, smiling and panting with excitement.

"This is so wonderful!" she exhaled.

"WONDERFUL?!" I screamed. "I ALMOST GOT KILLED!"

"But that's the wonderful thing! Now at least we know that they're really trying to do you in and not just get the CD."

For a moment, I had to pinch myself to see if, indeed, the van had actually creamed me on the pavement of Seventh Avenue. Nope. I didn't see myself lying in the road separately from my spirit. No hissing devils dragging me to the bowels of Hell. Nope, I was sitting here in Dante's Inferno amid rolling clothes racks, cursing deliverymen, and honking horns.

I decided not to call Detective McMillan about the road

kill accident just yet—I couldn't stand another round of swarming policemen, another round of questions, and more warnings to watch my step without the benefit of police protection.

I took a cab back to my office and began thinking that today was a total waste until I listened to my voice mail and found that I had received a message from a frightened-sounding Frank Addams. It seemed that he wanted to make a deal for the pictures. A big deal. Half a million dollars, in fact.

"**A** half-million dollars!" Monette shrieked into the phone in her office. "Jesus, I could semiretire now . . . until I figure out what to do with the rest of my life. Maybe a small cabin in Vermont. Of course, I'd have to split the money with you, but then I'm so desperate to get out of the Endangered Herbs Society of America that I'd have to kill you and take your half."

"Monette, I thought just last week you said the job had its *moments*."

"Yeah, moments—lasting just moments. No, it's my boss, Hardcourt."

"Him again? I thought he was calling you his best friend just a few days ago."

"Well, yes, the borderline loved me a few days ago, that is until I killed a plant."

"Killed a plant! For God's sake! Plants kick and scream when I take them into my apartment because they know it's the Green Mile for them: their last gasp."

"It wasn't just a plant. It was some sort of thyme that was almost extinct. Someone sent it to the office to transfer it to the botanical gardens, but we kept it overnight. Since they were fumigating the office at night, Hardcourt asked me to take it home because he had other plants to rescue."

"Monette, I'm sensing that this story doesn't have a happy ending."

"It doesn't. I put the plant on the stove when I came home, and forgot about it. I put some lasagna in the oven to warm up and I ended up frying the plant."

"Monette, it's too bad you weren't cooking turkey, because the thyme would have gone with it nicely."

"Don't laugh. I'm in serious trouble with Hardcourt."

"Oh, tell Hardcourt to stop getting his Batman cape twisted into a knot. You said the plant is almost extinct. Tell him to get another."

"He can't because that *was* the last one. It's now officially extinct. I, Monette O'Reilley, friend to animals and all things living, registered Democrat and a vegetarian as long as I'm dating one, has wiped a living species off the face of the earth. My cat won't even speak to me now."

"Did she ever before?" I asked.

"No, but I can tell she hates me. She left a turd on my running shoe two days ago and she won't come out from the closet to greet me anymore. I tell you, word has gotten around."

"I'd steer clear of Central Park for a while. The squirrels are probably planning an ambush."

"I gotta find some way to make it up to Hardcourt. I need to be in his good graces because my yearly raise is coming up for review. How much did Frank say he'd give us for the pictures?"

"Now, now, Monette. Blackmail will never get you anywhere, except to the first floor at Tiffany's."

"So what did Frank sound like when he called?"

"Monette, he sounded really serious on his message. And get this—he was actually apologetic for the way he treated us. He pleaded for us not to release the pictures."

"Did you tell him to stick his head up somewhere the sun don't shine?"

"No, when he told me that he'd part with half a mil for those pictures, I wanted to call him and tell him something else."

"And what would that be?" Monette ventured.

"Sold!"

"Don't think about it, Robert. People like you and I were not meant to do those things, mainly because we look too guilty and we get caught. People like Michael have no morals. Doing this kind of stuff comes naturally because they can't imagine getting caught or being denied anything."

"Oh, Monette, after Frank's call, I did a little researching on the Internet and guess why Frank is so willing to hand over so much money for the photos."

"Because he doesn't want it known that he's unkind to models?"

"No, because he has an IPO about to happen."

"An initial public offering? You mean someone is about to give that daffy queen a bunch of money in exchange for stocks in his company?"

"Yes, Monette. To the tune of two hundred and fifty-seven million dollars."

"No!"

"Oh yes. He's going to branch out into home furnishings, cars, luggage, even baby strollers. When Frank is done, this country is going to look like everyone is on active duty. So what should we tell Frank?"

"What do you mean, what should we tell him? We tell him we don't want money, but we're not releasing the pictures, either."

"Can't we just ask for a little money? Like, fifty thousand. He'd pay that without thinking about it. He probably spends that much on eyebrow pencils each year."

"Robert?"

"Yes, Monette?"

"I'm going to hang up the phone now and call you right back. When you pick up the phone, I want to be talking to the lovable, neurotic Robert Wilsop that I remember."

"Wouldn't you rather be talking to the slightly wealthy Robert who can afford to take you out to great dinners and send you away to lesbian summer camp?"

Monette, never one to make idle threats, hung up the phone with a polite, but firm click. Exactly three seconds later, my phone rang.

"All right, all right," I sputtered into the receiver, "we won't shake Frank Addams down for the money, even though he is a prissy loudmouthed butt wipe who deserves to have every horrible piece of clothing he's ever made shoved down his fat little throat . . . his fat, fat, fat throat."

"You're absolutely right," Monette agreed, although it wasn't Monette's voice: It was Frank Addams.

"Holy fuck!" I said to myself. "Oh fuck, oh fuck, oh fuck!" I again told myself—as if once wasn't enough.

Frank was overlooking my little faux pas because we had something he wanted. "RobertIknowIdidn'ttreatyouand Monetteverywellinmyofficetoday.Iwanttomakeituptoyou two.Howaboutsomethingfrommyclothingcollection?"

I couldn't picture myself in an orange and red stretch chemical warfare suit, nor could I do the same with Monette. I politely declined the offer.

"Look Frank, Monette and I don't want anything . . ." I started to say, but stopped myself. "What I began to say was the only thing we want are straight answers to a few questions."

"Straight?You'reaskingthewrongperson.I'msogayIcan't eventhinkstraight."

You could almost hear the snare drum rim shot: pa-rump-pump-pump.

"No money, but I want to remind you, if you don't answer the questions we ask you, you'll be on the Internet faster than naked pictures of Brad Pitt."

"Anythingyouwant.Justholdontothosepictures," he pleaded.

"I will call you back in a while, Frank. I have to talk to Monette. How about tomorrow, twelve noon?"

"Ican'tIhave . . . no,twelvenoonitis."

Frank had a well-deserved reputation for being difficult, but I'd underestimated how much he wanted those pictures because he'd acted so nonchalant about them at lunchtime. Once he got over himself, he must have realized how much damage the pictures could do to his career.

As soon as I hung up, the phone rang again. I decided this time to make sure who I was talking to before I assumed anything.

"Monette?"

"Of course it's Monette. Who did you think it was?"

"That's the problem. I thought I was talking to you and it turned out to be Frank Addams."

"So did you give him our message?"

"Yes, I did. Then I also did some fast thinking. I told him we wanted to ask him some more questions and that if he didn't give us straight answers . . ."

"To which he replied, "Baby, I can't even think straight.""

"Something to that effect. You must be clairvoyant."

"Not really. It's easy to predict the predictable."

"Oh, right," I replied. "Anyway, Frank said he'd see us at twelve noon tomorrow."

"Great! What do you have on tap for tonight?"

"I think I will just stay in at Michael's, watch a movie on TV, and go to bed. I'm trying to lay low."

"Sounds like a plan," Monette said. "I'll meet you downstairs in the lobby of Frank's building at eleven forty-five tomorrow. Tonight, I want you to draw up a list of questions that you think we need to ask. We'll compare lists before we go up see him."

"There's only question I want to ask him," I replied.

"And what's that?"

"How long would it take you to get half a million dollars in unmarked bills?"

"I thought we decided that the money thing is a dead issue."

"I guess so," I admitted. "Well, I'll talk to you tomorrow morning at work."

"Sounds good. Bye."

I hung up the phone and thought to myself: What's the real dead issue here—the money . . . or me?

10

I Enjoy Being a Girl

"Half a fucking million dollars and you're not going to take it?" Michael shouted. "Just for giving some queen with a sewing machine a CD with some pictures on it?"

I knew it was a mistake to mention our current situation to Michael since his view on the subject would coincide with mine—an occurrence that rarely happened. The last thing I needed right then was to have someone vehemently agreeing with my idea to take the money and run.

"Robert, if you don't grab that money, you're a fool. I mean, what can happen? Addams is not going to tell anyone about the pictures because he wants to keep things quiet. You give him the CD, take the money, and go buy yourself some decent clothes."

"So why are you so vocal about the money, Michael? You have all you could ever want."

Michael looked like I had just slapped him across the face. "That shows just how little you understand about having money. *No one* could ever have all they could want. And for your information, you know my setup. My mother has control of the Stark purse strings. And furthermore, I can barely get by on what she sends me."

"Michael, you get over fifty thousand a month."

"Yes, Robert, but I have expenses most normal people don't. My co-op fees are outrageous! Last month, one of the building's elevators broke and you should have seen the bill! Everyone in the building is going to have pay for that in raised fees, and since I have the apartment with the most square footage, guess who gets hit the worst?"

"Michael, *you* broke the tenant elevator when you made the deliverymen use it to take that metal sculpture up."

"How was I supposed to know it weighed one ton?"

"Michael, don't make excuses. You get away with breaking most of the building rules because you have the most votes in the building. Besides your penthouse, you bought several apartments in the building just so you could have more votes on the co-op board."

"That's not illegal. Leona Helmsley does it all the time!" Michael protested.

"You don't know that, Michael."

"But I bet she does," Michael spit back.

"Michael, your conjecturing is too easy. I could probably say that Leona stabs people, eats their brains, then tosses their bodies into a human-size grinder and makes them into hamburger that she has cooked and served up for her and I'd probably be right."

"Well, all I can say is take the money or you'll regret it."

"Michael, we're not taking the money."

"Can I then?"

"Michael!" I was actually shocked by his comment, which was shocking in and of itself since almost nothing that Michael did could shock me anymore.

"Just give me the pictures, we'll get the money, and I'll split it with you, sixty-forty."

"It's really stupid of me to even ask this, but I assume the sixty percent is not my share but yours?"

"That is correct."

"So why do you get sixty percent? The pictures were given to me."

"Because I'll take the blame if things get messy. I get paid for taking the extra risk."

Feeling that this conversation—like most that I ever had with Michael—was going nowhere, I tried to finish so I could watch some television.

"Well, Michael, I've got to get to bed. I have to come up with some questions to ask Frank Addams."

Michael picked up an expensive knickknack from his coffee table and examined it with dull eyes. "Why don't you ask him why he likes to dress up as a Pamela Anderson in need of a good electrologist?"

I was amazed. "Michael, how did you know this about Frank?"

"I saw him at a fetish party at Jim Hitchcock's in January. He likes to be forced to wear ladies' lingerie with stiletto boots in black vinyl. Crotchless fishnet stockings when he's in the mood. Definitely *not* my trip."

"Michael, why didn't you tell me that you saw Frank Addams before?" I asked, only too late to realize that I already knew Michael's answer.

"No one asked me."

"Michael, what else do you know about Frank Addams?"

"He was doing the forced-girly-thing long before he met up with Cody Walker."

"How long ago? And with whom?"

"Oh God, years. Years. See, he was making the circuit of all the sex parties long ago. I guess he never thought he was going to be a big designer someday, so he had no problem flaunting his sexual turn-ons in front of everyone. He started as a drag queen, then I guess it grew into what he's into now."

"So, Michael, let me ask you a question. Frank hired Cody to . . . well . . . you know . . ."

"No, I don't know, Robert," Michael said, baiting me to say what I had trouble saying.

I refused to step in that pile of poo. "You know what I mean, Michael."

"No, Robert, I really don't. Tell me. You have to be more specific." A devious smile played across his face.

"Tie him up and stuff."

"Robert, it's called SM. Listen, if you're going to be silly enough to turn down Frank's generous offer and go asking questions about this whole mess, you've got to call things by their proper name."

"Michael, I didn't go to school at a whorehouse. I grew up in the Midwest, where we didn't talk about such things!"

"Robert, calm down . . . you're starting to hyperventilate. It's just sex. People everywhere have kinky sex. You think that because you came from the Midwest, no one ever did anything besides vanilla stuff. I'll bet the farmer next door was boinking the farmhands on his tractor or nude-wrestled them in the mud."

"Michael, I grew up in the suburbs outside of Detroit. We didn't have tractors."

"Okay, combines or whatever those mechanical corn-picking things are."

"Michael, this may come as a shock to you and other New Yorkers who think there's nothing west of the Hudson River besides San Francisco and Los Angeles, but we had electricity, indoor plumbing, and lived in houses built from real bricks and mortar and not mud."

"Robert, I've been to the Midwest before."

"When?"

"I've changed planes in Chicago many times. Isn't that

the place where they're always wearing down coats and snowmobile boots?"

"Yes, and we're all proud of the fact that we trap our breakfasts every morning."

Michael smirked.

"Oh, Wilsop, I forgot to mention . . . I saw your porn debut on the Internet today. You're all over. Nice work. I didn't know you were uncut."

"Michael, could we get back to the subject of men in crotchless fishnets?"

"Fine. You lead . . . it's your dance."

"Okay. Frank's fantasies seemed to require a dominator. Did he have someone who played that role before Cody?"

"Yeah. A guy named David Bharnes."

"Is there some way I can contact him?"

"I could give you his phone number," Michael said nonchalantly.

"Michael, you didn't . . . !"

"Oh, for God's sake, Robert. Can you imagine me being submissive to anyone on this earth?"

"Other than your mother, no."

"I'd just approach this guy carefully. Don't go telling him you want to ask him questions about a murder—he'll shut up like a clam."

"Well, pray tell, how should I approach this guy? On bended knee?"

Michael looked at me and smiled a lecherous grin. "That would be a good start."

The next day, I met Monette in the lobby and showed her my list of questions. She studied them carefully, then proceeded to cross off the bulk of them with a heavy black pen.

I felt like I was back in third grade with my teacher, Mrs. Lacie, who took personal offense at my penmanship and made me practice my 1s and 7s hundreds of times on the chalkboard until my knuckles were bloody.

"Monette, what's wrong with my questions? Are they that bad?"

"They're just not focused. You see, in order to solve a crime, you need to devise a theory of what really happened, then you ask questions and chase clues that support that theory."

"Okay," was all that I could muster in response.

"Fine, let's go see Peter Pan."

And up we went in the elevator, with me trying hard not to picture my favorite childhood storybook character in crotchless fishnets. As the elevator ascended, I couldn't help but feel that Monette had been a little harsh on my questions. I resolved to show her—somehow.

We were ushered into Frank's office. He was actually smiling, actually looked at us, and was . . .

"Sowhatdoyouwanttoaskme?" he started.

I was about to say that Frank might actually be speaking slowly enough to understand him without intense concentration—but two out of three ain't bad. Monette pulled out her query list and began to question him—that was, before I stopped her cold.

"Frank," I started, "tell me about David Bharnes."

Frank turned as white as a Pratesi sheet.

"Mymy," he said as he twiddled his thumbs. "You*have*been busy!" Frank admitted. "DavidBharnesandIhaveplayedbe-fore.Manytimes."

"Did David ever take pictures of the two of you?" I continued. Monette, taken aback at first, now let me pursue my own line of questioning.

"Yesyeshedid."

"But you're not worried about those?"

"No."

"Why?"

"Hedoesn'tgoshootinghismouthoff.Plus,hedoesn't takepicturesunlessmyfaceiscovered."

"So David would never stoop to using those pictures for blackmail?"

"Nohe'snotthatkindofguy.PlusIthinkhekeepsallhisphotos lockedinabigsafe."

"I see," even though I didn't. "I have another question, Frank. You said you had these *sessions* with David many times. Was there something special about David?"

"Hewasgood.Heplayedalongandmadeitwork—what everyouwanted."

I was on a roll now. "If David was so good, why did you switch to Cody?"

"Davidsaidhewasn'tdoingthatsortofthingformoneyany- more,thoughthat'snotwhatIheardthroughthegrapevine.I've heardhe'sstillactivebutjustnotwithme."

"Those are all the questions I have, Frank," I said. "Mon- ette, do you have any questions to ask Mr. Addams?"

Monette was dumbfounded. She started to shake her head, then blurted out a question.

"Frank, on the night of the murder of Eric Bogert, where were you?"

"Smokingonmybalconyandwatching*ValleyoftheDolls*."

It sounded like an airtight alibi to me for any gay man.

"The whole night?" Monette inquired further.

"Yesyesyes."

"Did anyone see you . . . to corroborate your story."

"Justthecuteguyintheapartmentbuildingacrossthestreet."

"Thank you, Frank. You've been most helpful."

"OhMissO'Reilley,couldIhaveyourworkphoneincaseI thinkofsomethingimportantlater.IhaveRobert'sworkphone butI'dliketohaveyours."

"Sure," Monette complied, writing her work phone number on a piece of paper for Frank.

"Thanks.IfIcanbeofanyhelpdon'tforgettocallme," Frank said as he smiled widely.

As soon as we were safely in the building lobby downstairs, Monette turned to me and patted me on the back.

"You done good in there, partner," she said. "Once I saw what you had dug up and where you were going with it, I trashed my questions. Yet another confirmation that Eric was probably doing the blackmailing, and that Frank is sticking by his shaky alibi that leaves him unaccounted for on the night of Eric's murder. So where did you find out about this Bharnes guy?"

"Where do you think I get sex information?"

"Michael! Of course!" Monette said, slapping her forehead. "I should've known. We've got to find out more about him and what he knows about Cody and Eric. Do you know where we can contact him?"

"Yes, Monette, but there's one problem."

"And what's that?"

"Michael told me not to go questioning Bharnes because he won't reveal a thing."

"So how does Michael propose getting information out of this guy?"

"He didn't say, but I'm afraid it's going to involve me wearing a dog collar."

11

Robert Scores!

"Hello, David Bharnes?" I said nervously into the phone. "I've been referred by Frank Addams. He told me that you could help make some of my fantasies come true."

There was a short silence on the other end of the phone that stretched off into eternity. I could almost feel his antennae reaching out, scanning me, and sizing me up over the copper wires.

"Frank, eh?"

Was David putting me on the spot by saying nothing, letting me get nervous so that I would blather endlessly, exposing my fear and gauging my honesty and sincerity? Or was I letting my paranoia get the best of me? It was hard to tell . . . I was entering new territory.

"Yes, Frank. He spoke in total confidence to me, since he knew that I was cool."

Oh shit, I thought. *Cool*. That, in itself, should expose me as a pretender. *Cool* is exactly what a faker like me would say, trying to sound worldly and easygoing. A novice like myself wouldn't say words like *cool*. I should be nervous, apprehensive. I've blown it, I thought to myself. I was ready to scream and hang up the phone then go hide in a closet when I did the sensible thing.

"Mr. Bharnes. Could you excuse me a second. There's someone at my door. Could you be so kind as to hold the line a second?"

"Yes, certainly," came the voice on the other side of the receiver.

I put the phone on mute then slapped myself across the face. Then again. It was only then that I could pick up the phone.

"I am so sorry for the interruption, Mr. Bharnes. Now, where were we?" I asked.

"Frank," came the short answer.

Jesus, I thought to myself. This guy wasn't going to give an inch, was he? Well, at least he wasn't going to be any good at verbal humiliation—he couldn't seem to speak more than a word or two.

"Yes, I was telling Frank about my fantasies, and he said I should get in contact with you."

"Perhaps. Maybe you should start by telling me your name."

I had no intention of using my real name. Not only was I shy, but I was getting to be known around town, both as the holder of the treasured sex CD and now as the Guy Who Can't Zip Up His Pants.

"My name's Brad Willoughby. You still fulfill these kind of fantasies, don't you?"

"I might. Tell me what you're looking for, Brad."

Shit. I didn't expect to be asked this question so early on. I thought we'd meet for drinks or I'd go to some oily car re-pair shop in lower Manhattan, where he'd ask me a litany of questions. Q and A, if you follow.

I looked around my room in Michael's apartment for some kind of straw to grab on to. Nothing. It was difficult to imagine that I was staying in Kinky Sex Central and I couldn't think of a thing. Just when I thought David was going to hang up on me as simply another crank call, I saw something. Next to my bed was the picture of Monette that I had brought with my few other belongings during the exodus from my apartment on the Upper East Side. Monette was in her Leaping Lesbians of Park Slope soccer uniform, holding the trophy that I had, ironically, chucked out the window of her apartment a short time ago trying to thwart a burglar/assassin and that had been creamed by a passing cab. Life's a bitch then you get flattened.

"I'm into soccer fantasies," I blurted out.

"I see."

"Yes, soccer uniforms."

"And Brad, what do you fantasize about doing while you are wearing this soccer uniform?"

"I, uh . . ." I stuttered, not knowing where to go from there.

"C'mon, Brad, you can tell me what you want. There is no need to be ashamed or uncomfortable with me. I have worked with many men and seen many things."

I looked at the picture of Monette again. She was holding the trophy in one hand and had a soccer ball underneath her other arm.

"I'd like to be tied to the goal posts and have someone kick soccer balls into my groin," came the answer before I had the chance to think about what I was saying. Shit. Okay, think fast. Cover yourself—literally. "And I'm wearing a protective cup at the time."

In a few seconds, I figured the vice squad would break down my door and arrest me for unspeakable perversions, but the response I heard from the other end of the telephone line was rather comforting.

"Oh, *that*. This is a very common fantasy, Brad. There is no need to feel that what you desire is out of the ordinary."

This was very weird. When I called, I had visions of having kinky sex in a garbage-strewn alley with prostitutes looking on, their scabby lips and torn pantyhose bearing witness as I had tawdry sex atop garbage cans while rats and cockroaches vied for supremacy at our feet. But this was nothing like what I had expected. I felt like I was sitting in a comfortable Park Avenue office full of Oriental art and rugs—and David Bharnes was a Jungian analyst.

"Well, thank you, Mr. Bharnes. Could we meet to play out my fantasy?"

"Did Frank mention that my services aren't *inexpensive*?"

At hearing the words *aren't inexpensive*, I, like most New Yorkers, assumed we were talking fees that only royalty and captains of industry could afford. But I had to have answers, and answers didn't come cheap. This was my life I was talking about.

"Frank said that you hadn't seen each other in a while, so could you illuminate me as to your fees?" I proposed.

"Eight hundred an hour. Cash. Upfront."

We were back to skanky prostitutes in raunchy alleys. Cash. Upfront.

I winced and said okay. Eight hundred dollars! I would make it short. One or two kicks and I'd hightail it out of there.

"Excellent," David said. I formed a mental picture of him sitting in a leather-bound wing chair next to a roaring fireplace and tenting his fingers in a display of Victorian horror that only Vincent Price could emulate.

"How about tomorrow at nine P.M.?" I asked.

"That sounds fine. Come to 101 1/2 West Broadway, loft number five. Bring your gear in a gym bag, and BE ON TIME!" David shouted. "You understand, Brad?"

For some reason, I answered automatically, "Yes sir!" My

answer startled me. Was it something in the distant-yet-com-manding presence of David Bharnes, or was it some hidden persona inside me that I'd wanted to release for a long time?

I sat in the gathering darkness of my room in Michael's apartment and wondered if I were beginning a long day's journey into night. But at the same time, I wondered why I was titillated at the same time?

"Michael, I need some advice—and I need you to keep an open mind about what I say."

Michael looked at me as if I had told him that I belonged to a neo-Nazi organization bent on destruction of the world as we knew it. I told him what was about to happen tomor-row night. I advised him to sit down.

"What the fuck are you telling me?" he yelled exasperat-edly. "You're going to wear some soccer clothing and have a guy kick soccer balls into your groin and you think that's kinky!? God, Robert, are you boring!"

"Michael, I'm not as sexually experienced as you are!" I explained. "I don't have a proctologist and urologist on call twenty-four-seven like you do."

"They're not on call twenty-four-seven, Robert! They're on *retainer!*" Michael spat back.

"My mistake, Michael. Just give me some pointers," I begged.

"Robert, I can no more teach you how to have wildly ex-otic sex than Michelangelo could teach an orangutan how to paint. It's a gift that you have, or you don't."

I decided to whine a bit. It's worked before. "Michael! I don't know what to do."

"Robert, I know that this is going to sound like outra-geous advice, but JUST BE YOURSELF!"

"But I don't want to! If I'm myself, I won't have any fun!" I said back.

"Holy shit, Robert! What would Freud say?"

"What?"

"Robert, you just said that you wanted to have fun."

"I did not," I replied in the best tone that would convey that I was absolutely certain of what I had said, even though I quickly realized my Freudian slip was showing.

"Oh yes you did!" Michael laughed.

"Okay, maybe I did. But what I meant to say was that I wanted to *look* like I was having fun so that my character would be convincing."

"Robert, you go ahead and tell yourself whatever you like, but the cat is out of the bag. You have a kinky side."

"Michael, you know the only fantasy that interests me is having Russell Crowe play Phalus Maximus the gladiator with me."

"He's married now," Michael added.

"I know. Pity. I guess I can take consolation in the fact that he's not happy with his wife. I can see it in his face. It's me he really wanted. I just know it."

"Now we really are talking fantasy here," Michael quipped.

"Oh shut up, Michael. If you'll excuse me, I'm going to call my boyfriend in Palm Springs and tell him that I'm going to cheat on him tomorrow."

"Hello, Marc?"

"Yes? Oh, Robert! God, I've missed the sound of your voice. How are things going?"

I decided to tell Marc straight out. "Marc, I'm going to cheat on you tomorrow."

"Okay, so how did you get Russell Crowe to leave his wife?"

I wondered if Michael's apartment had been bugged. "Funny you should say that, because Michael and I were just talking about him."

"The gladiator thing?"

"How did you know?" I was astonished at Marc's psychic abilities.

"You told me that one night you were out here and got drunk on margaritas."

"Oh," I replied. "I didn't say anything else embarrassing, did I?"

"I'm not telling you, Robert. I'm saving up that ammo for when we have our first big fight. So what's this about you having an affair on me?"

I confessed my plan to Marc. He didn't get angry. No shouting. Not even a veiled threat about stalking me for days then jumping out of the bushes and blowing my head off. Nothing. The guy was emotionally mature. "Go ahead—you have my blessing!"

"So you're not angry?" I asked just to make sure.

"No, Robert. This is something you feel you have to do."

"Well, now that you're practically tossing me at this guy . . ." I replied.

"Robert, listen. When you were here, you and I connected like long-lost soul mates. We're now thousands of miles apart—but the connection is still there. If you told me you wanted to go out and experiment a little, I'd say go ahead. Robert, I want you to grow as a result of us being together. What I don't want to do is stifle you and stunt your growth. Simone de Beauvoir once said about her forty-year relationship with the existentialist Jean Paul Sartre, that wasn't it amazing that our lives have coincided for so long?

I interpret that she saw the bond between them as something that was held together by strengths, not weaknesses. And when it was necessary to part, that she would do so. That's the way I see a relationship—all relationships, in fact. I don't believe in Barbie and Ken heterosexual relationships where high school sweethearts see each other across a crowded room, fall in love instantly, and live happily ever after. I can't think of anything more revolting. People change in a world that's constantly changing around us. Everything is so dynamic. Go, try things, experiment, become the most Robert you can be! That's my definition of love: helping you become the most Robert you can be. I can't define love as 'Oh Robert, you make me feel secure' or 'I need you.' That all sounds so selfish. I'd rather help you and be giving to you. It's not all about me!"

I wanted to burst into tears right then and there. What Marc had said was so mature, so inspirational, I couldn't believe I had snagged a guy this good. Before I met him last Easter, all I could see was an endless stream of losers, freaks, psychopaths, and sociopaths. Like almost every single gay man in America, I wanted someone intellectually challenging, capable of helping me grow and vice versa. I wanted this so badly, and like many gay men, I jumped at a lot of bad choices because I was so desperate. And just when I was about to give up my search and move into a nunnery, Marc picked me up—literally—and threw me in a pool in Palm Springs, clothes and all. Love comes looking when you least expect it.

"Marc, I just love you so much."

"And I love you, too. And Robert?"

"Yes, what is it, Marc?"

"If you fall for Soccer Guy, I will crush your balls in a vise, then drop-kick them all the way to the state line with steel-toed boots."

"Oh, gosh," I gushed, "Marc, I love you too!"

"Just be careful," Marc warned me.

"Believe me, I have to be. No matter how you look at my situation with you and Soccer Guy, it looks like I'm going to get a kick in the balls regardless of what happens."

12

The World Cup

I stood patiently outside a dusty-looking loft building in Tribeca, having pressed the door buzzer. I waited fifteen thousand years for an answer. Or was it three seconds? Time had warped out of existence as I stood there watching the flow of cars going uptown, carrying their payloads of corporate ants north toward apartments on the Upper West and Upper East Sides.

"Yes?" came a voice so suddenly that it almost made me jump backward into the street.

"Brad Willoughby here. David Bharnes?"

"Yes, of course. Fifth floor. Take the elevator at the end of the hall . . . on your right."

The door buzzed and I pushed it open to reveal dark, dingy hallways that looked not unlike those of my decrepit apartment building on the Upper East Side. As I trudged down the hallway toward the elevator, I fought that little voice in the back of my head that told me to run away; you don't know what you're getting yourself into. I got in the elevator and pressed five. The ancient contraption contemplated whether to ascend or stay put so long, I pushed the five again. Then again. Then again. Satisfied that it had exacted some sort of revenge on me by pushing some of *my* buttons, the elevator ground upward, delivering a neck-wrenching jolt as it passed each floor. When it reached the fifth floor, the door rolled back and the elevator went into a stupor. Or perhaps it was paying homage to its master, David Bharnes, having delivered another victim into his gaping jaws.

There was only one door on that floor—straight down the corridor I was now traveling. At this point, I was glad I had left my whereabouts on a sheet of paper on the kitchen counter in Michael's apartment. If anything happened to me, Michael would tell Monette, who would set in motion a chain of events that would end with a team of four thousand SWAT officers dropping from airplanes, rapelling down from the building's roof, and climbing up the walls of the loft building with suction cups on their knees. I would be safe.

I knocked on the door and waited. To pass the time, I looked down at my leather gym bag, which was filled with soccer clothing that I would probably end up wearing only once in my life—in the next hour or so, to be exact. I was studying the tiny creases in the leather when the door opened.

The thing that startled me about how the door was opened was the fact that it wasn't kicked open in surprise like a police raid. Nor did it creak open slowly, pulled, no doubt, by a desiccated mummy hand with long fingernails grown over thousands of years in a granite sarcophagus in lower Egypt. No, this door just opened like I was being welcomed to a Park Avenue terrace cookout with Mitsy Binkerman.

The man holding the door open was none other than Sean Connery. Or at least that's what he looked like to me. He was in uniform already, his soccer shorts a little tighter than would probably be allowed on playing fields at the World Cup. I guessed his age to be about fifty-five, judging from his salt-and-pepper hair (for which I have a distinct weakness) yet he had a remarkably athletic body, the leg muscles nicely toned, his forearms strong and capable. He was, like Sean Connery, distinguished looking—even in his soccer gear.

"Come in, Robert," he said, shaking my hand in a very gentlemanly manner. Gone was the gruff exterior I had expected. At any moment, I assumed that he would invite me to sit in a leather wing chair and have a Montecristo cigar and a snifter of priceless brandy. I couldn't imagine that in a short period of time, this erudite and urbane man would be firing soccer balls into my groin. As I've always said, life is a contradiction.

As he invited me into the loft, I was struck by another contradiction: The loft, instead of being littered with filthy, stained mattresses and sordid sexual instruments, more precisely resembled a Hollywood storage warehouse. There were legions of clothing hanging on rolling racks all around the cavernous space. Football uniforms, doctors' white coats, Greek Spartan warrior getups as well as uniforms from the U.S. Marines, other branches of the military, and police departments from around the United States and the world— even superheroes: Spiderman seemed to be the most numerous, followed by the homoerotic gear worn by the caped crusaders in the last round of Batman movies. Scattered around were also things that could only be considered props. Rifles (did they really work?), ambulance stretchers, lockers, locker room benches, spears, horse saddles, cowboy lariats, gloves— even a mechanical bull. I began to feel very prudish.

"Mr. Bharnes, before we—" I began to say, but was cut off.

"Mr. Willoughby, I know that you're new at this, but before we begin, I ask all my clients to pay up front."

"I understand," I said as I handed over an envelope containing eight hundred of my hard-earned dollars. What the hell—it was only money.

David opened the envelope, made a cursory count of the bills inside (fifties), and put it into a back pocket of his shorts. "Good, shall we begin?" he said. "You can put your sports kit on in that room there."

"Sports kit?"

"That's what the Brits call it. I have several clients that have been in the World Cup. Mostly the Brits—they're some of the kinkiest people on earth. Followed by the Dutch, then the Germans."

"Oh, well, that must be wonderful," I managed to reply. What else could I answer to such a comment? On the world tour of kinkiness, I had definitely missed the bus. "Mr. Bharnes, David . . . I'm new at this, so could we take this slowly? Could we talk a bit beforehand?"

"Certainly. Brad, I get a lot of novices and a lot of them like to talk first. It helps to break the ice."

The two things New Yorkers never tire of talking about are real estate and what they do for a living. I guess I could have quizzed David about his loft space, but I was more interested in the fact that someone did what David did for a living, and seemed to live quite well by it. My interest was more than just an attempt to shed some light on the Case of the Airborne Bodybuilders, but another desperation that I had in life: the desperation to get out of advertising and do something that didn't so closely resemble the life of a dung beetle.

"So I can see you've had a lot of experience in this?"

"Movie stars, TV people, church bigwigs . . . since I was thirty. Twenty-five years ago. You do the math."

"So I guess you've seen just about everything, huh?"

"Brad, your fantasy is about the tamest thing I've done for some time."

Was this a compliment, or more confirmation that I was a prude? "Well, I have to compliment you on the way you make it comfortable for guys like me."

"Like I said, I've done this for a long time with a lot of men."

I wanted to be careful not to push too hard, too fast, for fear of tipping David off as to my real intent.

"Actually, a friend of mine, Michael Stark, said that Frank Addams was a client of yours for a long time."

No visible emotion.

"Was," David replied. "I turned him over to Cody Walker and Eric Bogert. They're dead, you know. Killed themselves or someone killed them—does it matter? What a shame."

The way David said his last sentence, it was clear he didn't really think the loss of two hustling bodybuilders was such a terrible thing.

"Nasty competitors, I guess?"

"Cody and his steroided friend, Eric, strong-armed me into giving up some of my clients. Now that the papers say he was blackmailing society-list gay men, I'm not surprised that the two of them got murdered. You don't mess with some of those guys."

"So lots of rich, powerful men come to you?" I asked, then realized most of my questions were sounding like, well, questions. I needed to divert attention from them. "Don't get me wrong, I'm not asking you to name your clients . . . it's just nice to know that I'm in the hands of the David Bharnes whom the rich and powerful trust for discretion . . . and a good time."

"Those that haven't been wrenched from me," David replied.

Wow. Despite David's remarkable coolness and self-control, he was angry enough to spill some dirt about two people he didn't think I knew.

"That's terrible!" I said in true sympathy. "I'm sure you go to great lengths to get clients—and their trust—and someone comes and steals them away. That's just not right."

"I have a black belt in karate, but you can't stand up to a two-hundred-eighty-pound mountain of muscle in a roid rage—they're homicidal, just crazy. Enough about me. Should we get started?"

It was clear that David felt he had told me enough already and was ready to get back to business, which was fine with me—I had learned a very valuable piece of information.

"Could we talk a little more first?" I asked, hoping that I could talk my way out of my fantasy and go back to my temporary home in Michael's apartment.

Hours later, I entered Michael's apartment, and crossed the living area on the way to my bedroom, but was surprised when the Eames chair facing the television spun around quickly.

"Robert!" Michael greeted me. "Monette called but I told her you were out somewhere. Why are you doubled over like that?"

"I got a little too big for my britches, Michael. Why didn't you tell her where I was?"

"How was I supposed to know? I don't keep track of your whereabouts."

"But I left you a note in the kitchen, Michael. A very important note!" I explained.

"There wasn't any note in there!" Michael complained as he got up to go to the kitchen to prove how wrong I was.

I followed just to show him I knew what I was talking about.

We both entered the kitchen, and like Michael claimed, there was no note on the counter.

"I left it right here," I said, jabbing the countertop that had somehow eaten my note. "I know I did."

Michael went over the trash and retrieved a piece of paper and handed it to me. "Is this what you're babbling about?"

I looked at the note: *"James 9" uncut 555-8793.*

"Michael, I didn't write this!"

Michael grasped my wrist and turned my hand upside down so I could see the other side of the note: *Michael, I will be at David Bharnes' tonight in Tribeca—it's not what you think. In case I disappear, call the police.* I should have known that Michael would do something like this. I was about to take him to task for treating my note so contemptuously, but I relented. After all, I did return alive.

Michael smiled at me. "I guess David didn't kill you. But it looks like you suffered a slight injury there, Robert," he said, patting my crotch lightly, from which I jerked back. "Take my advice, Robert. The next time you do this, wear a little foam padding inside the cup. That's what I always do."

13

To Catch a Thief

The next morning at work, I was about call Monette to tell her what had happened last night—parts of it—when the phone rang. It was Monette.

"How did the meeting with David Bharnes go, Robert?"

"Oh, pretty well. I found out that—"

Just then, the receptionist beeped my phone.

"Monette, can I put you on hold for a minute?"

"Fine, I'll be here doing a layout on cardamom pods."

"What?" I said, confused on every front.

"Never mind, Robert. I never do or I'd go crazy."

"Okay, Monette, I'll put you on hold for a second. Yes, Lisa, who is it?"

"Michael Stark."

"Did he say what he wants?"

"He'd rather not say—but he did tell me it was highly embarrassing and that it was important."

"Okay, I'll take it, Lisa."

I waited, and in a few seconds, Michael's laughter exploded out of the phone.

"So what's so funny, Michael?"

"You are—or at least your balls are. You're all over the

Internet. The U.S., the United Kingdom, I even found pictures of your testicles on a German website where they put embarrassing photos. You're right next to a Berlin zookeeper who got shit on by an elephant."

More laughter.

"Michael, thank you for telling me this again because what I really need in my life right now is to know I'm the object of global ridicule. I'm in the middle of a meeting, so I've got to go."

"Oh, Robby, before you go, why didn't you tell me you had such low hangers?"

I disconnected Michael and went back to Monette.

"Monette? You still there?"

"I'm here. So what did Michael have to say?"

"Oh, nothing, Monette. Absolutely nothing."

I was interrupted again by another call from Lisa at the reception desk.

"Yes, Lisa. It's not Michael again, is it?"

"No call. Something just arrived for you here. It's out at the front desk."

"Who's it from?"

"Frank Addams . . . on Seventh Avenue."

"Lisa, I'll come out and get it later. Could you mark it so no one else takes it? You know what thieves those art directors can be."

"I won't let anyone take it, Robert. Anyway, there's a big sign on it that has your name written in four-hundred-point type."

"Okay, I'll be out later." I retrieved Monette back from the land of hold. "Monette, you there?"

"Yes."

Another beep signal from the front desk.

"Yes, Lisa, what now?"

"A Detective McMillan on the line, he says it's important."

"Thanks, Lisa," I replied. I clicked over to Monette. "Monette, could I call you back? McMillan is on the other line. He says it's important."

"You will call me if it's an emergency, won't you?" Monette pleaded, the concern in her voice making me concerned.

"You know I will—gotta go," I said and hung up the phone. "Lisa, could you put the call through?'

"Right away."

I didn't know what was going to happen, but I couldn't imagine that it was going to be good.

"Hello. Robert Wilsop here."

"This is McMillan here. We have good news. We had your apartment staked out in the hope that someone would try and get in again, and we got our man."

"You caught the person who burgled my apartment?" I asked. It was too good to be true. Could this case be over already?

"We've got a man in custody at our station. We want you to come by as soon as you can to see if you can identify him."

"But Detective McMillan, I never saw who broke into my apartment."

"This isn't a lineup. Maybe you saw him standing around your place, maybe you saw him at the gym."

I agreed, but I wasn't quite sure what I had agreed to. However, I was curious to see who broke into my apartment. Maybe with victim restitution laws, I could force the asshole to clean up my apartment and alphabetize my magazines again. As I went into the lobby to catch an elevator down, I saw a rack of women's clothes—frilly, shiny numbers that only a loose woman would wear out on the town when she wanted to be fucked by it. I glanced at the clothes absentmindedly until I saw the huge tag that boasted my name. I ran over to look at the tag. At the bottom, after it said in screaming foot-high letters, *For Robert Wilsop*, was a short handwritten note that said, *Gotcha!—Monette.*

The elevator door opened behind me and I dashed for the elevator in an effort to get downtown, hopefully to wrap up this mystery and get on with my life. As the elevator entered freefall, it occurred to me that I could've had Lisa roll the rack into my office, or into a closet so that everyone in the agency wouldn't see, but then I thought fuck it. I was completely *out* at work, so why did it matter? Plus, I could always tell people it was for a photo shoot.

I rode downtown to McMillan's station and stood in the lobby, waiting to be escorted to his office. It's strange how you can feel so unsafe in the midst of so many policemen and women. There were criminals everywhere—the kind you don't see in the cleaned-up crime shows on television. These guys looked like they had not only stabbed their families to death, but eaten them as well.

McMillan came out and led me down several corridors to a room that looked out, presumably, through a one-way mirror to the burglar sitting there, handcuffed, in a chair facing an empty desk. It was none other than Chet Ponyweather, uberWASP. I couldn't believe it. Civilized, impeccably bred Chet. Prep schools, Ivy League, and now detained in a shabby police station, handcuffed like a Wall Street investment banker who'd advised Martha Stewart to do a not-so-good thing.

"Do you recognize this man?" McMillan asked, scowling at Chet as if he had just been caught selling crack to two-year-old blind paraplegics.

What to do, what to do. If I said no, I might set the wheels of justice spinning backward. If I admitted that yes, I had not only seen the man before, but had actually visited his office to question him about the murder of Cody Walker and Eric Bogert, McMillan might not look too kindly on my—our—investigations ("Monette put me up to this," I was prepared to squeal). Despite the pros and cons, I decided that honesty is always the best policy. So I admitted that I had questioned him at his office.

"WHAT THE FUCK ARE YOU TELLIN' ME?!" was McMillan's quiet reply. "YOU QUESTIONED HIM AT HIS OFFICE! WHAT ARE YOU, FUCKIN' CO-LUMBO?"

I was thinking that Monette and I had more of the charm, sophistication, and wittiness of Tommy and Tuppence of Agatha Christie fame, or Hercule Poirot and Miss Lemon, his plucky and efficient secretary. But *fuckin' Columbo?* This just showed how McMillan, despite his devilishly rakish looks, couldn't think outside the box of pop television programs.

"Why don't you tell me what you and Monette have been doing behind my back? You two could have gotten killed snooping around! Someone is serious about this matter. They've killed two guys who could probably bounce the bouncers at most bars in New York. Don't you understand? This isn't some sort of murder whodunit weekend in Bucks County! They chloroformed two guys and threw them off balconies . . ."

For such a seasoned professional, I couldn't believe that McMillan would let slip a piece of privileged information like that. Chloroform. Hmm. McMillan must have been really angry to let that pussy out of the bag.

"Oh, never mind," McMillan said finally. He turned

away from me to stare once again at Ponyweather, then he did the most extraordinary thing: He turned back, grabbed my hand, and held it.

Under the normal, paranoiac circumstances that compose what I laughingly call *my life*, I would have expected that McMillan was about to slap cuffs on me and drag me kicking and screaming to the bowels of the building where they beat confessions out of prisoners. But no such thing happened. Without even looking at me, he stared straight ahead and said, "I just don't want anything bad to happen to you."

To say I was stunned would have been understating the moment. It was surreal. Yes, that was the only word for it. For years, I have chased lunatics trying to land a decent date, and when I find a mentally stable guy in Palm Springs and get, effectively, taken off the market, the men come out of the woodwork. I would have no more thought that McMillan was gay than the man in the moon, but here I was in a darkened observation room with his hand grasping mine. Truth is stranger than fiction. You just can't make this stuff up.

He released his grip on my hand and turned to look me in the eyes. Yes, he meant what he had just said to me. I just couldn't believe this was happening to me. Me. White boy with no sense of rhythm whatsoever, from Michigan, had a hard-talking New Yawk detective in love with him. It was like Stephen Hawking and Ginger Rogers: the pairing just wouldn't make sense. But in a crazy universe, this had happened. It was happening. There was no denying it away. No ignoring it. No escape. Curiouser and curiouser. You didn't have to disappear down a rabbit hole to experience this lunacy—it was my life!

"Well, Luke, I thank you for your concern. It's nice to

know that you really care for my safety, and I'm not just some case to you." I picked up his hand and squeezed it back, then let it go. I didn't want to lead him on, but I wanted to let him know I appreciated his concern from the bottom of my heart. But then I thought, would I be committed to going to dinner with him? Then what? Sex? No, cops look at life differently. They like to go to a shooting range before sex. Bang, bang, thank you, ma'am. I then decided that I was thinking too much.

The only thing left to do was to spill my guts about what Monette and I had been up to. McMillan, with the exception of a few cringes and some saucepan eyes as I hit some exciting points, listened attentively to what I said, obviously impressed by what two amateur detectives had uncovered so far.

"Okay, listen, Robert—and Monette, wherever you are. I will let you do some investigating—on one condition: that you inform me before you do anything. And I mean *anything*. I think that by applying pressure from different directions, we can force the killer out in the open. But my hunch is that this investigation is going to go quiet for a long while. The guilty party is going to know that the police are crawling all over this case right now. To make a move right now would be foolish."

"Correct me if I'm wrong, but Chet here didn't seem to let a little publicity prevent him from trying to break into my apartment to get the pictures."

"You are correct, Robert. The guy was so desperate, he was trying to jimmy your door open with a crowbar. Hardly the professional sort, huh?"

"Certainly the desperate sort, however. A crowbar, huh?" I asked. So crude, it seemed, for a man so refined.

"He made a lot of noise, so your neighbor down the hall

looked out her peephole, saw Chet, and called the police. Because your address is marked, if there's a call on it, I get alerted."

I looked back at Chet again. "Has he said anything?"

"He's asked for his lawyers, so we won't get anything out of him for a while. But we questioned him yesterday about Cody and Eric's deaths. He denies that he could do such a thing, but here he is breaking into your apartment a day later. What I don't get is how he knew where you lived."

"If he didn't get my address from the newspapers, radio, or television news, I am, stupidly, in the phone book. I've taken my name out of directory assistance, but I can't do anything about the phone book. I'm sure all he had to do was look me up. Dumb, huh?"

"Not really; lots of people choose to have their phone numbers listed. I wouldn't be too hard on myself."

"Detective McMillan, you're talking to the wrong person. I am a self-contained masochist and sadist—all rolled into one. I can do something, punish myself for doing it, and enjoy it."

McMillan seemed unconvinced. "You, naw!"

"Listen, Sister Elleanor McCardle used to give me gold stars for being the first kid in our class who could properly flog himself without using a mirror."

McMillan laughed, for what I think was the first time. Did his handholding start a thaw on that frozen exterior of his?

McMillan turned to me suddenly, proposing a thought. "Let's pool our resources. You tell me what you know and I will let you in on a few things."

"Your offer sounds great, but it doesn't seem quite equal."

"I can't let out too much—my job, you know. You've got

to be discreet with every piece of information I give you," he whispered while giving my hand another quick squeeze.

I smiled back at McMillan. "Yes, but why let us in at all? You don't even know us."

"Oh yes I do. I've gone through the case files on some of the escapades you, Monette, and Michael have been involved in. You have quite an interesting life, Robert. Murder in Provincetown, Berlin, and Palm Springs."

"I like to keep busy. Weird, huh? I'm a white bread Midwesterner who should come no closer to a real murder than Laura Bush to a gay-pride parade. But there it is. I blame it on an evil vortex that I picked up on a trip to Sedona, Arizona, years ago."

"The vortexes there are supposed to be about energy, not good and bad."

"That's what they tell you there, but they saw me coming. They had this bad vortex they wanted to get rid of, and they attached it to me on my disastrous trip there with a crackpot boyfriend by the name of Fuckhead. I think this witch put the hex on me when I complained that she overcharged me for a crystal I bought for Monette in a shop in town. I knew something was up when all the photos I took of the area came out blank. On the trip back, the baggage door on the plane opened on takeoff and we had to abort and return to the terminal. Seven hours later, we left Phoenix and the skywaitress spilled a tray of drinks on me and I flew back to New York wet with Sprite. I rest my case."

McMillan snorted a short, gruff laugh at my theory. "I guess I shouldn't be standing next to you now. A meteorite might come crashing through the ceiling and hit the both of us."

"I wouldn't kid about that if I were you. That's my number one fear. There's a meteor out there and it's got my name on it. So, changing gears here, why in the world would Chet try something so stupid as to break into my apartment?"

"Desperation," McMillan said without skipping a beat. "People do stupid things when they get desperate."

"So why do it yourself?"

"Again, desperation. And being a WASP."

"What does being a WASP have to do with it?"

McMillan looked at me like I was born yesterday. "I can't imagine that this guy knows anyone who would pull off a burglary for him."

"No, but I bet he knows plenty of people who can make paper-thin cucumber sandwiches. Anyway, I get your point, Luke."

"Exactly. So let's go somewhere and you can tell me what you've found out," McMillan said, grabbing me by the arm and ushering me out of the room and out of the building. "The City of New York will pay for your cup of coffee."

Why not? The only thing I had to look forward to at work was the package brochure for the new feminine hygiene pad our agency was helping our client launch. Nobody came into our agency to work until 10 A.M. anyway, and after that, it was catch as catch can to find people who seemed to drift in and out the agency on spurious missions. ("I HAD to go to Bloomingdale's to check on their window presentations," a TV producer would protest. "The reason I was at the Armani boutique all day was because I was looking for some sweaters for my models in an upcoming photo shoot," another art director would offer.) So, I went and flirted with disaster again.

We sat in a Starbucks as McMillan paid for my grande iced coffee of the day. We sat down, surrounded by kids pecking at the keyboards of laptop computers or reading cryptically named novels written by unpronounceable authors.

I told McMillan about our questioning Frank Addams; Chet Ponyweather; Eric's girlfriend, Adrianne; and even David Bharnes, whom I covertly referred to as Marvin Gardens to protect his identity.

McMillan then told me what he knew, and it was the choicest piece of information I could have hoped for. Of all the clients on the CD-ROM I received, only four had questionable alibis at the time of Cody and Eric's death. Frank Addams was one: He told police what he'd claimed during our visit—that he was alone, chain-smoking Marlboros on his balcony and watching *Valley of the Dolls* on videotape. Chet Ponyweather said he had taken a long walk from his Fifth Avenue apartment and returned several hours later. Allen Firstborn, who visits sinful New York City regularly, claims he was praying to the Lord at his *eight-room* pied-à-terre on Central Park West. Another suspect was the Republican mayoral candidate, George Sheffield. Besides having a fondness for wearing infant clothing as part of his fantasy, he claimed he was doing a political fundraiser dinner which, it just so happens, he didn't attend. The only suspect that wasn't under a cloud of suspicion was John Bekkman, who was out of town backpacking and whose story checked out.

McMillan's cell phone rang. From what I could overhear, someone else had attempted to break into my apartment and the scoundrels had been apprehended. Two of them. It was officially open season on my apartment. Monette and I figured that only someone desperate enough to kill would be desperate enough to break and enter someone's apartment. We were tragically wrong. McMillan hung up.

"Two amateur thieves hired to do the job by none other than Frank Addams, the designer. They were paid ten thousand each."

SHIT! For fifty thousand, I would have gladly given the pictures to Frank myself and he wouldn't have put himself at risk. But kind, considerate, moral Robert tries to do the right thing and ends up with nothing. Once again, life had confirmed the fact that bad guys finish first—and richer.

McMillan's phone rang again. He answered it then handed the phone to me.

"For me?" I asked.

"It's Michael Stark."

I looked at the detective quizzically and shrugged my shoulders.

"Michael, why are you calling me on Detective McMillan's cell phone?"

"Because you refuse to get one."

"Yes, Michael, but how did you get the detective's number?"

"I went through all your personal things and found his business card."

"Of course," I replied. "I forgot that my personal belongings are yours by divine right."

"I wouldn't say it exactly like that, Robert. Oh, by the way, you're getting low on razor blades. And condoms. You know, Robert, you should check the expiration dates on your rubbers. It looks like you've had them in your shaving kit for a long time. Funny thing, the box has never been opened."

"Michael, is there a reason you called me on an official police phone?"

"Yes, could you meet me for lunch?"

"I'm downtown, Michael—talking to the detective about the latest tour bus that tried to break into my apartment."

"Great, you're close by to me. We could go to Assembly."

Considering the day I'd been having, I decided that at least I could go to lunch and treat myself. Or rather, work a miracle and have Michael pick up the tab.

"Okay, Michael, I'll meet you there at twelve-thirty. Now I have to get off the phone."

I hung up and was about to hand the phone back to McMillan, but asked him if I could make one important phone call.

McMillan nodded and told me to go ahead.

"Hello?" I spoke into the phone when someone picked up on the other end.

"Lisa, this is Robert. Robert Wilsop. I'm really feeling crummy, so I'm going to take the rest of the day off and get some sleep. Would you see that everything's covered? Oh, and one last thing, could you push the rack of clothes for my next photo shoot into my office and shut the door?"

14

Robert and Michael Get Taken for a Ride

I met Michael and we had a great lunch. We had great service, wonderful food, saw Diane Keaton sitting at a nearby table, and even treated ourselves to a great bottle of champagne. Everything was going so well. All was right with the world—until I tried to get Michael to pay.

"Robert, I'm running short until the end of the month. Could you pick up the tab and I'll pay you back?"

I should have known better. Michael did this all the time. What was worse, I fell for it all the time. No matter how you looked at it, I was the worst codependent personality since Patsy Cline. Instead of considering myself as being self-contained and having all that I needed to be a whole human being, I hung around Michael because he did exciting things. At least that's what my therapist Bethany said. And she was right. If only she had given me some more sensible advice. If she had told me to leave my wallet at home when dining with Michael, I would have put her in the category of genius.

Speaking of wallets, the thought that mine had been stolen by some reporter a few days ago just occurred to me.

I had spent the last of my money taking a cab to the restaurant.

An hour later, Michael had managed to cajole the president of the Stark Foundation into paying the bill with his credit card. The president had to, in a way. Although Michael had a terrific no-show job at his family foundation, the president was supposed to keep tabs on Michael's work hours and report them to Michael's scheming mother at her lair in Newport, Rhode Island. But Michael, who resented anyone telling him what to do, had turned up some dirt on the president after hiring a detective firm to have him followed. From that moment on, Michael had the president in his coat pocket.

Although the bill was paid, it didn't solve how we would get across town to Michael's apartment. There was no choice but to walk. Michael, who spent forty-five minutes every day, five days a week, on the treadmill at the gym, howled like a banshee when he found out that we would have to hoof it. As a last resort, I suggested going into the subway and illegally hopping the turnstiles, but I realized how far-fetched my idea was the moment it left my lips. I had known Michael for a long time and he had never taken the subway in his life. In fact, he said that the only thing that should be running through tubes under the pavement is sewage. So we walked and Michael made what could have been a very nice trip across town in the spring sound like the Death March to Bataan. As he went on and on about the indignity of having to walk like a proletarian, I noticed a long, black limousine that was crawling along the street, matching our walking pace. In New York, where limousines are a common sight, you don't pay attention to them, unless, that is, they come to a stop thirty feet ahead of you and two guys built like linebackers in suits get out to beckon you to come closer. Were they the two guys who had chased Eric off the balcony of his apartment a few days ago?

"Mr. Sheffield would like to talk to you," one of the men yelled to us.

I thought about turning around right then and there, but Michael grabbed my arm and pulled me toward the car.

"C'mon, let's see what this is all about. The one on the right is hot," Michael whispered in my direction.

From the time that I was old enough to go outside by myself, my mother warned me not to go near cars with strangers in them. This sage advice has guided me past danger from the time I was a child to the time a man circled my car in Grand Rapids, Michigan, flashing a fan of five hundred dollars at me—indicating my minimum wage for a night's pleasure. But for Michael, the danger suggested by something hidden behind tinted windows was too alluring to him not to resist—not that we had much choice. The two suited men stood like Spartan sentinels channeling us in the direction of the open door. I suppose that we could have made a run for it, but the suits looked like they might not only be powerful, but quick on their feet.

We approached the car and Michael got inside with not even a second's hesitation. Me, I bent over to look inside to figure out what I was getting into. Sitting inside was none other than George Sheffield, the Republican candidate for the mayor of New York City.

"Get in, Robert," he beckoned. Seeing my hesitation, he spoke up gruffly. "Oh, for God's sake, Mr. Wilsop, I'm a public figure! I'm not going to abduct and kill you two . . . especially with the Democrats watching my every move, so get in—I'll give you a lift."

I got in and sat down. One of the suited guys closed the door and both got into the front with one driving and the other riding shotgun.

It was the first time that I had seen George Sheffield up close, but I was struck at how sinister he seemed. No spring chicken he, George had that dried, desiccated, rubberized look of Charleton Heston. His frame was lanky and clothed in a conservative pinstripe suit designed not to look too *with it*, but you could tell that it had been made by the likes of Oxxford or Hickey Freeman. No Armani for this guy— Democrats and freethinkers wore that kind of suit. The most frightening feature on George's face were his eyes; the tiny black pupils were set so deeply inside his red, bloodshot eyes, it looked as if he spent his days laughing as he tossed widows into the snow from the hundreds of apartment buildings he owned. (I imagined that when George had the unfortunate timing of evicting someone in the dead of summer, he probably had snow carted in from northern Canada just so he could throw the unfortunate slob into it.)

"Mr. Wilsop," George began, "I know that you've been trying to get in touch with me about some . . . uh . . ." He looked over at Michael, who was already pouring himself a martini.

"You don't have to worry about him," I replied. "He's seen the pictures and knows all about them."

George smiled a crocodile smile. "Ah yes, nothing is secret in this town . . . unless you want it to be."

"You thirsty?" Michael asked me, holding up an empty martini glass to tempt me. "It's Grey Goose Vodka from France. It's supposed to be pretty good, but I have my doubts about what the French know about making vodka— or a decent car for that matter."

"No, no thank you . . ." I said, then reconsidered—I should profit at least a little bit from the trump card that I still held. "On second thought, Michael, I will have one."

Another crocodile smile and a knowing glance. If I were a zebra, I would have bolted from the watering hole after a look like that.

Sheffield fixed me with his gaze, and began what I figured was a canned speech used over and over again to intimidate anyone foolish enough to stand between him and something he wanted to possess. "Mr. Wilsop, as you know, I am a wealthy man . . ."

"I'm aware of that, Mr. Sheffield," I replied.

Another interruption from Michael. "A martini, Mr. Sheffield?"

"No, no thank you, Mr. Stark."

"Mr. Sheffield, if you don't mind me asking, how is it that you know my name *and* Michael's? And how did you know we'd be walking down the street at just this moment?"

"As I told you before, Mr. Wilsop, there are no secrets in this town."

I was beginning to get mad with this cat-and-mouse game. I mean, who did this guy think he was? Goldfinger?

"You didn't answer my question, Mr. Sheffield. I asked how did you know it was us? You're evading the question like a true politician."

I got a snort of laughter from George this time.

"Robert, there are a lot of people in this town keeping a watch on you and your movements. That includes Mr. Stark here, too."

Michael stopped sipping his martini and looked at it closely, trying to determine if it was poisoned. Perhaps it was. I put mine down just in case.

"Are you threatening me, Mr. Sheffield?" I said, anger rising in my voice.

"I am doing nothing of the sort, Mr. Wilsop. I'm just saying that it wouldn't be a wise idea to try and do *anything* with those pictures. You'd make a lot of enemies in this town if you did."

I thought of throwing my drink in George's face right then and there, but pity stayed my hand—it would be a pity to waste good vodka.

"Meaning the two guys in the front seat might push me off a balcony without my consent?"

"Them?" George said, pointing with his eyes to his two henchmen sitting on the other side of the soundproof glass behind us. "They wouldn't hurt a fly!"

Sheffield chuckled to himself again—a chuckle that ended in a phlegmy gurgle deep in his throat. He was clearly enjoying himself.

I again reconsidered the martini glass in my hand. It would make a good missile. No, no, I said to myself—not yet. I decided to take a different tack.

"George, you said earlier that you were a wealthy man."

"Yes, Mr. Wilsop, what are you getting at?"

"I'm not suggesting anything," I said, forging ahead. Two could play this game. "Several of the men whose pictures are on that compact disk offered me a lot of money in exchange for turning it over to them."

This time, a great cackle from Sheffield. "Are you trying to blackmail me?"

"No, nothing of the sort. I'm merely telling you that others have made me some very generous offers," I explained. "Michael! Would you stop tapping on the window, trying to get the driver's attention!"

Michael looked hurt, but his libido was never bruised.

"I see, Mr. Wilsop. I think that the only thing you will reap from this affair is trouble . . . even here in New York City, this bastion of petty little Democrats."

It was time for *my* crocodile smile.

"Thank you for saying that, Mr. Sheffield," came my reply.

"Why would you thank me, Mr. Wilsop?"

I took a sip of my martini.

"Because, Mr. Sheffield, the police have me wearing a wire. Your conversation is now recorded for the police—

and the incumbent mayor to hear. Thank you very much for the ride, but Michael and I have to get out now." I took another sip of my martini, then threw the remaining vodka in George Sheffield's face. Sheffield looked stunned that anyone would dare do such a thing. And to be perfectly frank, I was stunned, too. It was just that I was getting fed up with this entire ordeal.

Sheffield ordered the car to stop, and Michael and I got out. Michael still had his martini glass in his hand, which I grabbed and carelessly tossed into the backseat of the limousine, contents and all. For my finale, I slammed the door so hard, it sounded like it would come out the other side of the car. The limousine pulled away from the curb and slunk away with its muffler between its wheels.

Michael, stunned that we had to *walk* again, reached out and shook my hand.

I looked at Michael in equal amazement. "What was that for?"

"For standing up for yourself. The way you talked back to Sheffield, you'd think you had as much money as I do."

"I'm sure it emboldens you when you have a buttload of money, Michael."

"Partly, but it also helps to be diagnosed as narcissist-borderline-histrionic personality. But never underestimate the power of having *fuck-you money*."

"Is that what you call it, Michael? Fuck-you money?"

Michael looked at me and cracked a big smile. "Can you think of a better name?"

"Frankly, no. I just wish you could tell me where I can get some of that currency."

"Robert, just because you told off that old coot doesn't mean you're going to get me to vote for the Democrats."

"Michael, your voting is something I will never understand. Why do you do it?"

"I vote with my pocketbook. The Republicans are the party of the rich. I'm rich, so I vote for it."

"You vote to protect your money?" I asked, aghast.

"Of course, what other reason would there be for voting Republican? Their hypocritical moralizing and social policies are atrocious."

"Michael, you have an army of tax lawyers and accountants that help you avoid ever having to pay a penny in taxes. What about all the conservative judges the Republicans are getting into federal seats? Laws prohibiting gay discrimination will take giant steps backward. And gay marriage will never be approved!"

"For crying out loud, Robert! What gay man in his right mind would want to get married?" Michael retorted with horror. "The whole point of being gay is that you can sleep with anyone you want, anytime. Why are these politically correct gays always trying to force us into adopting the hetero lifestyle and sell us the virtues of living in cute little bungalows with picket fences and monogamous relationships? I like being able to sleep around and sample different men. Why are people always trying to pee on my parade?"

Overlooking Michael's unfortunate and pathetic metaphor, you could now guess that Michael's political leanings were driven by the two great forces in his life: his libido and his checkbook. Traditional political labels didn't apply here. Michael was what you would call a conservative slut. Because of his beliefs, he was accustomed to offending people in some of the most egregious instances, which, personally, I think he enjoyed. It was the *power thing*. He liked knowing that he could get a rise out of people and it didn't matter that it sometimes meant occasional hardships for him. For instance, the tires on his Hummer were routinely slashed by eco-terrorists, members of animal rights groups routinely hurled drinks and insults in his face because of the exotic and endangered animal skins that were turned into elegant and expensive footwear on his behalf, and neighbors on Fire Island never forgave him for the time he almost swamped one of the ferries full of queens when he raced past it in a rented yacht at full speed in order to be first into the dock on a Friday night. Let them eat cake.

"Could we take a cab, Robert? We've done enough walking."

"Michael, it's, like, ten blocks to your apartment. Plus remember, we still don't have any money."

"But—"

"Walk, Michael. Remember how it works? One foot in front of the other until you get to where you're going."

Michael grumbled and groaned, but gave in reluctantly.

The pedestrian walk light had just come on for us and we were preparing to cross the street when a car came around the corner with such ferocity that there was little doubt of its intention: The driver meant to run us down. But being seasoned New Yorkers, we waited that extra millisecond, knowing that running stoplights was a popular local sport, especially at the beginning of rush hour. It all happened so quickly that we didn't have time to be scared or even shocked—it just happened. The one thing I did take note of, however, was that the vehicle was not a blue van.

"That guy tried to kill me!" Michael exclaimed.

Me. Kill me. A narcissist to the end.

"Michael, I think he was out to get the both of us," I reminded him.

"Oh no he wasn't. He was after me. Fuck! I wish I hadn't sent those e-mails . . ."

Something was rotten in the state of Denmark and it wasn't their stinky cheeses.

"Michael, what have you done?!" I demanded.

"Nothing."

"Yes, you did! You thought that car was meant for you. Why?"

"Well . . ." Michael said, hastily preparing a story in his feeble brain. You could almost hear the gears turning in his head. Clink, clink, clank, clunk.

"Michael!" I shouted.

"Oh Robert, you know how I am. I mean, me being kind of opinionated—I make enemies easily."

"Tell me something I don't know."

"Well, people try to kill me all the time, so when those two *incidents* happened the other day, I didn't think anything of it."

"What incidents?"

"A car tried to run me down. Twice. I guess that's why I hesitated in crossing the street just a few minutes ago."

"I noticed that. I also noticed that you let me go into the street just slightly ahead of you."

Michael reached over and playfully rubbed my head. "Aw, my trusty little human shield."

"Thanks for the flattery, Michael, but you haven't told me what you did to deserve this?"

"Will you look at that jacket!" Michael exclaimed about a leather coat in a storefront window.

"Michael!"

"Oh so what, so I made a copy of your CD and called the guys on it and asked for some money in exchange for the pictures."

Now I was shocked.

"Michael, how did you get a copy of those photos? I never downloaded the pictures to your computer."

"My computer recorded the keystrokes you used to get to your mailbox, and I just repeated them."

"Keystrokes?"

"Yes, remember that hot guy who used to clean my apartment?"

"Jake? The one who was arrested for wire fraud and grand larceny?"

"Yeah, him. I know he was using my computer to scam people, so I had some techie nerd install a program that records every keystroke someone makes, so later I could figure out what he was up to."

"So you followed my trail, downloaded *my* photos, and then used them behind my back to make money because you can't control your spending?"

"That's about it. Boy, you are good."

"Michael, if I didn't need a place to stay, I would have you drawn and quartered right in front of me for what you just did."

No words were exchanged between us for the next block or two, then I decided that Michael was Michael. It was foolish of me to expect anything else from him. The problem was that you couldn't anticipate how dastardly he could be. Or how stupid. Uh-oh.

"Michael, when you asked for money from these guys on the CD, you didn't give them your phone number or address, did you?"

"What kind of idiot do you think I am? My phone number—no."

"You didn't mention your address! You didn't!"

"How were they supposed to deliver the money to me? Oh, stop worrying, Robert. I live in a doorman building."

"Ferguson? He couldn't stop Stephen Hawking from getting past the front door."

"Oh, so what. You know what kind of security system I have in my apartment. Plus, the elevator doesn't stop at my floor unless you have a key."

True, Michael's apartment was armed with sophisticated burglar detection equipment that could sense a gnat crawling along a picture frame, but the catch was that you had to *turn on the system* in order for it to work.

We finally made it to Michael's building; passed Ferguson, who was staring blindly into space as Michael and I walked through the front doors (Michael was pissed that we had to open the doors ourselves); got into the elevator; and rode up to his apartment, where the doors opened on his floor, no key necessary. I made Michael promise to use the key from now on and to use the alarm system even when he was in the apartment.

I got on the phone and called Monette at her office, but she had already left for the day. I made Michael give me the copy of the CD he had downloaded and erased it. Then I used a hard drive scrubber to make sure what was erased stayed erased, then went on Michael's computer, erased the keystroke recording software, and changed the passwords on my mailbox.

By the time I'd finished, Monette called back. I told her about our encounter with George Sheffield in his limo and about Michael's pathetically amateurish attempt at blackmail. She, it turned out, had some news for me.

Allen Firstborn had finally returned a call to her and wanted to meet us tomorrow in a church on Lexington Avenue, where he'd be praying. Oh brother, I thought. Monette also said she had done some very heavy thinking about my predicament and something was not adding up, at least when viewed from the perspective that we had. Like thunder in the distance before the storm, I could tell something was going to happen. She was on to something, even though I couldn't quite see what it was.

I then called Marc in Palm Springs.

"So someone's tried to run you over twice, your apartment had been broken into umpteen times, you have a police detective who's got the hots for you, and you don't think I need to come to New York?"

"I can take care of myself, Marc. Really I can," I protested.

"Of course you can, and you've done such a great job already. Listen, something doesn't add up in this whole matter. It seems like it's one thing being desperate enough to break into someone's apartment to steal an incriminating CD, but it's far different to murder two people. I think there's something behind this that isn't clear yet."

"Like what?"

"I know! Maybe there's a ring of hustlers all connected by some organization of personal trainers. Maybe Gold's Gym is really Golddigger's Gym."

"You know, Marc, as outrageous as that sounds, you might be on to something," I agreed. "Killing two bodybuilders would be nothing to keep a huge prostitution ring secret."

"I don't know, Robert. There's just something not right about this. I lay there in bed last night thinking about what it is that bothers me. But believe me, I will solve this because I don't want anything to happen to you."

Awww, I thought. I felt all tingly inside. Then he proceeded to make me feel all horny inside, the details of which I will spare you, dear reader.

"Before I hang up, Robert, I just wanted to let you know how proud I am of you."

Another awww.

"For my bravery?" I asked.

"No."

"For my amazing intellect?"

"No.

"For what then?" I asked.

"Your fame."

I was completely confused. "My fame?"

"Yes, you're the only boyfriend I've ever had whose balls have been seen the world over."

15

I'll Pray for You, Your Assholiness

We met Allen in the Park Avenue Baptist Church of the Living Waters of Our Lord Jesus Christ, which was really on Lexington Avenue. We entered the church and wandered up the aisle like the two heathens we were and approached Allen Firstborn, who was praying like a madman (and looking out the corner of his eye to see if we were watching how hard he was praying).

"Allen, I'm Monette and this is Robert."

He shook his head violently to let us know he was coming out of a trance.

"Sorry, my fellow brethren. When I'm talking to God, I leave my body. It's so difficult to come back to this sinful earth."

Monette and I both looked at each other.

"Mr. Firstborn, does that ever work on anybody?" was Monette's slap-in-the-face retort, which I think was fair. After all, he started it.

"Monette, I'm not sure what you are getting at. So what can this Lord's servant do for you?"

"Well, for a start, you can tell us about these photos of you with a hose stuck up your bum."

"I'm still not sure what you're getting at," Allen responded with a great, big fake smile on his face.

"Don't tell me you were going to Cody Walker for therapeutic high colonics. From what we'd found out, you'd been playing doctor with Cody for some time."

There was a flood of crocodile tears.

"It started when I was a little child in God's eyes. My dear, sweet mother, God rest her precious soul in the arms of our most precious Lord and Savior Jesus Christ, gave me enemas to flush the demons from my bowels."

Monette was thunderstruck. "What was wrong with fiber?"

"The Bible says to honor your father and your mother," Allen admonished us.

"When they earn it," Monette responded dryly. "Allen, you are evading my questions completely, giving me some drivel about your sainted mother. We're sure that your visits to Cody Walker won't be looked at favorably by your ministry."

"Miss . . ." Allen began with a smile on his face that belied the fact that this guy was probably the undiscovered son of Hitler.

"O'Reilley," Monette supplied.

"O'Reilley. I met Cody Walker when he was a bullrider in Oklahoma City. When I found out he was here in the Big Apple, I was overjoyed at finding him after so many years. My visits to him were purely related to my ministry. I liked to think of Cody as the lost sheep in the parable told by our Lord. My only interests in him were to guide him back to the way of the righteous."

"Like you, since you're such a terrific role model," Monette cracked,

Both Monette and I were flabbergasted. Never since

Nixon publicly declared on national television that he was not a crook had such a blatant crock of shit been served up for public consumption. It was clear that Allen had already planned his story and rehearsed it carefully, fearing that he would have to repeat it to the press. Allen was one of those people who felt that if you repeated a lie often enough, people would eventually believe it. Allen should have been working for the Bush Administration.

Monette wasn't buying any of it.

"Mr. Firstborn, when Eric Bogert approached you for money in exchange for the photos of you and Cody—"

"Miss Monette, I was never approached by anyone for money in exchange for the return of any photographs of me. My feeling is that Cody was possessed by the Devil and he doctored those pictures so that it would look like me. You see, I tried repeatedly to turn Cody toward the light of Jesus, but he wouldn't stop in his attempts to seduce me. When I repulsed his advances, he turned on me. Cody probably knew that because of irritable bowel syndrome— from which I suffer—I had to undergo frequent enemas administered by my mother and he took advantage of my unfortunate condition with the help of some computer software like Photoshop."

This guy was endless. The guy had also done enough homework to conjure up an explanation for the photos that might be plausible to members of his ministry, the bulk of which no doubt regularly read the supermarket tabloids and believed that a hunter in Mississippi had mistakenly shot down a real angel from heaven, that former President Clinton had given birth to a secret alien baby while in office, and that Nostradamus had predicted Viagra.

Monette tried again, although I could see that it was useless.

"Allen, the night Eric Bogert was pushed to his death, you told police that you were praying in your palatial apartment."

"Miss O'Reilley, yes, I was praying. For world peace, and that our nation should turn back from its sinful ways and lead us back to the Christian roots that made our nation great."

I was going to ask Allen if he meant slavery, but thought it better not to get in a pointless argument with a man who had raised denial to an art form. I had wanted for years to advance my argument to a Bible thumper that if Noah collected two of each animal to board his ark, then does that mean that he traveled to the caves of Kentucky to rescue the blind cave-fish, which exists only there in the entire world, or how could Jonah have been swallowed by a whale, since the only whales that are not plankton feeders and could even open their mouths big enough to scarf down a Biblical figure, the sperm and the orca, are not native to the Middle East region . . . but I held my tongue.

"Was there no one with you," Monetta ventured on, "who could testify that you were praying all night and never left your apartment?"

"No, Miss O'Reilley, there was no one with me, except Jesus, who will be my witness."

Monette smirked at Allen. "So you were alone. Fine. I don't think we'll need to call Jesus in for questioning."

Allen was taken aback so much, that I actually saw him pull back physically in response to Monette's very mild joke. Believe me, she was capable of better.

"Shame on you, woman, for making jest of our Lord! Blasphemy like that will bring down fire and brimstone on the heads of *your kind!*" Allen was now on his feet, shouting, "An abomination in front of the Lord!"

Although Allen didn't say the *L* word, it was clear that he meant *Lesbian* with a capital *L*. This was the final straw for Monette, who exploded like Krakatoa.

"Mr. Firstborn, you and your whole goddamn church can go fuck yourselves!" Monette shouted as she grabbed my arm and pulled me out of the church. "I'd make it a point to buy the *New York Post* for the next few days because as soon as we retrieve those photos from Robert's apartment, your ass is going to be on the cover!" she added. "Literally!"

Once we were out of the church and walking down the street, I could sense that Monette had calmed down enough for me to speak to her.

"Fucking righteous asshole. We've got pictures of Allen with more medical instruments inserted inside him than Liz Taylor during a liposuction operation and yet I'm the bad girl!"

"Well, you did shout *goddamn* and *fuck* in church!" I said, bursting into laughter.

Monette joined me. It was sad, but too funny.

"You know, Robert, you can't take life too seriously or it'll get to you and you'll end up in a fetal position pissing on yourself," Monette proclaimed.

"No truer words have ever been spoken, Monette."

Monette was quiet for a moment, then spoke.

"You know what we need, Robert?"

"Hip-high waders the next time we talk to Allen First-born?"

"That too," Monette conceded. "No, I think we need to take a trip back to your apartment. There are a lot of things that you've told me that disturb me."

"The rent?"

"That's true. You're getting hosed for such a dump."

"Yes, well, it wouldn't be such a dump if people didn't help themselves to my place when it suited them."

"That, in a nutshell, is what's bothering me, Robert."

"What? The break-ins?"

"Just one, Robert. Just one in particular."

16

Monette and Robert See the Light

A half hour and a cab ride later, we arrived at my apartment building. We climbed the stairs, and as we approached the door to my dump, both of us knew instantly that something was wrong. From inside the apartment, you could hear two males voices talking to each other and pawing through my things and tossing them aside carelessly when they didn't find what they were looking for.

"What are we going to do?" I whispered.

"Call the police, I guess," was Monette's answer.

"But by the time help gets here, the guys will probably be gone."

"What do you want me to do, Robert? Burst in there and cuff 'em?"

"Well, no, but I'm so pissed off at everyone helping themselves to my stuff that I want to go in there, pick up a chair leg, and start breaking skulls."

"Okay, you just go in there, Mr. Terminator, and clean up the joint."

"Sorry," I apologized. "It's just frustrating that I'm torn between what I should do and what I want to do."

But a second later, my quandary was solved for me. The

door to my apartment swung open and Monette and I were staring at two men in their early twenties who were as surprised as we were.

No one moved an inch as we continued to stare at each other, waiting for the other party to make the first move. Suddenly, one of the two men shouted, "Let's go, c'mon, this way!" and pulled his partner up the stairs toward the roof. While it wasn't the wisest thing to do, Monette and I bounded up after them, Monette merely following me, rage pumping in my veins.

The twosome quickly unbolted the door to the roof and burst through it and ran out onto the roof. When Monette and I reached the doorway, we stopped for a moment to gauge the situation, which wasn't in favor of our burglars. They ran toward the building on the west side of mine, but soon discovered that it was several stories too tall. They then ran in the other direction and discovered the apartments next door were a good story shorter than mine. They stood at the edge of the roof, trapped like rats.

Monette and I walked slowly toward them, not sure what we were going to do when we reached them, but that was a bridge we'd cross when we got to it. As we got within fifteen feet of them, the taller one grabbed the coat of his partner and yelled, "Jump, we can make it!"

They jumped, but they didn't make it—technically. No, they didn't fall to their deaths like I secretly wished, but they tumbled down onto the rolled asphalt roof and crumpled like circus tents with their center pole removed.

"My leg, my leg!" one screamed.

"Ow, ow, ow . . . dear Lord, remove this pain!" the other screamed in agony.

Monette turned to look at me and I read her thoughts instantly.

"Allen Firstborn!" I said excitedly.

"Bingo!" Monette said. "His ass is now officially in a sling. Let him deny himself out of this one!"

We both hugged each other.

"Do you think we should call an ambulance?" I ventured.

"Nah," Monette replied. "Let 'em suffer for a while. "Let's go down to your apartment, have a beer, and then we'll call the police. They're not going anywhere with those broken ankles."

Despite having every reason to have the two fundamentalist burglars beheaded on the spot, Monette and I are not complete sadists. We did *eventually* call the police, who called an ambulance. They were carted away through a throng of reporters who had magically appeared after being absent in front of my building for the last few days. I hated to say it, but I was happy to see them again, getting a lead on a hot story that Monette and I were all too happy to start them on.

When everyone had left, Monette and I got to work.

I began clearing up some of the tornado aftermath that was left in my apartment, but my heart wasn't into it since I figured that, given another twenty-four hours, everything would be a Red Cross disaster again. Monette, however, was studying one of my windows with an intensity that only a crazy person could match.

"Robert, look at this!" she commanded.

"At what?" I asked.

"The window ledge!" Monette half shouted.

I looked closely at the window ledge for footprints, handprints, or metal shavings, but the ledge was as clean as a whistle.

"It looks as clean as a whistle," I commented.

"That's the point. The air in New York is filthy. Car, bus,

and truck exhaust—the ledge should be filthy like the others. Unless, Robert, you clean them regularly—something that I wouldn't put past your obsessive-compulsive tendencies."

"Clean my window ledges regularly?" I said with mild outrage. "What do you think I am, crazy?" Monette had some nerve. I folded my arms across my chest for effect. "So what are you saying? That someone wiped my window ledge clean?"

"Yes, I am."

"So you think someone came down from the roof, or up from below, and entered my apartment through this window?"

"I don't think—I'm sure . . . wait a minute!" she said, fingering the filthy window. "Eureka!" she said with a self-satisfied smugness. "Rub your finger across this spot," she ordered me.

I did and felt a tiny chip in the window.

"It's chipped," I responded.

"It's not chipped. It's been drilled."

"Drilled?"

"With a tiny diamond drill bit . . . and a cordless hand-held drill. See here," she commanded. "Robert. Go get a magnifying glass."

Once again, I did as was told and retrieved the glass from my upended office table.

"See where the hole is?"

I started to see the light.

"Monette, it's right near the window lock."

"Exactly. Someone was outside your window and drilled a tiny hole right here. Then, they probably inserted a stiff wire through the hole and pushed the window latch back enough until the window could be opened."

"Amazing," I said.

"It's an old trick an electrician taught me. You can do the same thing to the tamper-resistant glass cover on your electric meter. You drill the hole, then stick a stiff wire into the wheel that spins on the meter and it stops the wheel from spinning, and *voilà*, free electricity! You remove the wire on days they read your meter."

"So that's why you always leave the lights and the television on in your apartment!"

Monette smiled. "The cat likes to watch Bravo. I come home and she's in front of the TV napping."

"So you think that they used the same trick to latch the window again?"

"Not likely. I don't think the trick works so well in reverse. It's one thing to push the latch open, but a lot different to close it by pulling on the window—you might break the glass. It seems too difficult . . . I don't know."

"Monette! You're amazing! So I guess our next question is how someone got to the window ledge?"

I raised the window sash and looked several floors down to the ground below us.

I made a few observations. "It seems too far down to have a ladder. Plus, it would make too much noise. So I guess the only way was down from the roof."

Monette could see that I wasn't quite convinced. "You look skeptical about that route, Robert."

"I am. McMillan went up there and didn't find any sign of ropes being used."

"I think we should go up and take a look around."

"Good idea," I replied, and up we went. We looked around for any sign that ropes had been tied to the building's boiler chimney. Nothing. Nor were there any holes in the roof or spikes having been driven into the mortar to provide a place to secure a rope. After half an hour we went back down to my apartment and returned to the open window, staring up to the roof above us. Nothing.

Then, as luck would have it, a light shone down on us. Literally. The sun cleared the roof and illuminated the air shaft between the buildings.

"Eureka again!" Monette announced. "Look up at the bricks above your window! Quickly! The sun is moving fast!"

I leaned out the window upside down and there, against the light, were small, but noticeable pieces missing from the mortar between the bricks. A distinct pathway wound its way upward to the roof—or down from it, depending on your point of view. Then, in a flash, it was gone.

"The sun rays aren't hitting it anymore," I said to Monette, "but I did see it! So someone *did* come down from the roof!"

"Yes, they certainly did!"

"But we didn't see any rope marks anywhere on the roof. I know! Maybe there was a second or third person on the roof holding the rope while an accomplice rappelled down to my window."

Monette scratched her lava red head then shook it. "Perhaps, but I have another idea."

"Another way down? How?"

Monette grabbed me by the arm and pulled me outside the window again.

"See how close the next-door building is to yours?"

"Yes . . . oh, no . . . you're not going to suggest that someone shimmied down between the two buildings, wedging themselves step by step."

Monette smiled that smile of hers that she got when she solved the unsolvable.

"That's what I think!"

I was in a state of disbelief. "But that would mean, that . . . that."

"Exactly!" Monette pounced. "Go on."

"That would mean that the perpetrator was an extremely agile person. Like a cat burglar."

"Or . . . ?"

"Like in Cirque de Soleil. A circus!" I said, sitting down.

"Yes, it's worse than we think." Monette said, shuddering as if a raven had just walked across her grave.

17

Send in the Clowns

Monette slunk down in a chair like a person fainting in slow motion. Fortunately, she had the foresight to place a chair underneath her. Circuses, if you don't know either of us, are the one thing that strikes terror in our hearts, but for different reasons—reasons that you will soon understand.

"I think Cirque de Soleil is behind this," I said. "They won't forget that incident when they came to New York years ago. Remember?"

The incident that I just mentioned was, without a doubt, the most humiliating moment of my life. Monette and I attended a Cirque de Soleil, mistakenly getting front-row seats. If you've ever seen one of their shows, you'd know how they have a comic ringmaster who gets on stage now and then and pantomimes between acts to give the cast time to prepare their costumes and accommodate scenery changes. This clown loves to pick someone out of the audience and make them play along with some act. Well, this one grabbed me and tried to take me up on stage, but I kept pulling away. The crowd was roaring with laughter. When I started walking back to my seat, the clown grabbed my arm and I pulled it back good-naturedly. Well, the clown slipped on some water left from the last act and he hit his head on the floor and was out cold. It was all completely innocent, but from the audience's point of view, I had hit the clown and knocked him out. The audience started booing me. Some of them even gave me the Roman Coliseum thumbs-down gesture. I got back to my seat next to Monette and she was sitting there in a state of shock.

My unfortunate encounter with clowns pales in comparison to Monette's. From an early age, Monette had developed a mortal fear of clowns that was equaled only by her fear of sauerkraut. The fear of clowns came from a childhood trauma she experienced at her third birthday party. It seems that her mother hired a clown for entertainment, not realizing that Mr. Happy the Clown (an unfortunate choice for a clown's name, I think), was a bitter man and a heavy drinker. During a lull in the festivities, Monette chanced upon Mr. Happy drinking from a flask behind a party tent staked out in her backyard. When he refused Monette's request to share in some of the *Kool-Aid* with which he was whetting his whistle, she playfully pushed him, knocking his flask to the ground and spilling out his precious whiskey. Mr. Happy, being about four minutes away from an attack of the delirium tremens, was in no mood to have his mental safety net drained away by a precocious, redheaded whatnot. He removed his big, floppy shoes and chased Monette around the yard with them, threatening to "pound her into the ground with them until she reached China." Mr. Happy, however, underestimated Monette's speed and agility, always following Monette by a good thirty feet. Then Fate and Betty Crocker intervened. Slipping on a piece of cake dropped on the grass by an easily distracted three-year-old party attendee, Mr. Happy hit the sugary mess and went down like, well, a drunken clown hitting a piece of cake lying in the grass. He lay motionless in the grass for some time, let out a loud gasp, his tongue shot out between his red lips, then he lay there quietly in the grass while Monette stared in horror from behind the trunk of a large elm tree. Monette's father emerged from the kitchen to survey what had happened in his two-minute absence. Prodding Mr. Happy endlessly, then feeling his wrist for a pulse, Mr. O'Reilley quickly concluded that Mr. Happy had donned his red nose and goofy wig for the last time. As if the chase hadn't traumatized Monette enough, seeing the alcoholic clown carried out of the backyard on a stretcher covered with a white sheet was the final nail in the coffin, so to speak. From that day on, she cringed at flea-market portraits of Emmett Kelley (but then again, who doesn't?), gave mimes a wide berth, and could be coaxed into attending Cirque de Soleil performances only while under the influence of five or six stiff gimlets.

As for the sauerkraut, the mystery would remain just that: a mystery. Monette was too terrified to speak about it and would avoid it in the same way that she steered clear of Oktoberfest—no matter where it was being held.

"Let's add everything up here. You had several break-ins to your apartment. The first one is extremely elaborate, owing to the press that was crowded outside your building."

"So does that mean that the other amateur break-ins by Chet, Allen Firstborn's minions, and Frank's hired henchmen get them off the hook as far as the murder is concerned?"

"Absolutely not. They all could've murdered in order to keep a scandal hushed up."

"But the only person who didn't clumsily break into my apartment was George Sheffield."

"*That we know of,*" Monette added slyly. "Maybe he was the first to arrive. You and I could be right in the middle of a mini-Watergate."

"You're not suggesting that the Republican Party is behind the murders and the elaborate break-in, are you?"

"I wouldn't rule it out."

"Shhhhiiiit," was all I could say.

It's one thing to find yourself drawn into a series of murders, but it's another when you find yourself in the middle of a conspiracy at some of the highest levels of the government. Was the CIA in on this? The FBI and the NSA too? Was I destined to vanish without a trace, my apartment inhabited by a look-alike and everyone who ever knew me silently erased? Or would I end up as a scientific experiment in some secret government lab, my head disconnected from my body and bobbing up and down inside a giant test tube, my body being used for DNA to build a master race of cyborgs that would take over the United States and make everyone wear hip-hugger stonewashed jeans?

I told Monette the theory that had just flashed through my brain. Wasn't it possible that there lurked some sinister organization in the background, I asked?

She was patting me sympathetically on the head like a good mental patient when she stopped in mid-pat and seemed transfixed at a point in space eighteen inches over my left ear.

"What, Monette, what is it!"

"You've just got me thinking of something."

"Yeah, what?"

"Just what you said: some sinister organization in the background."

18

A Huntin' We Will Go

Monette jumped on her idea right away.

"Robert, Michael's slept his way through just about every guy in town, hasn't he?"

"Yeah. In fact, he's actually repeated with some guys already."

"Michael also knows a lot of the gay elite in New York. Could you ask him to find out a few things about some people?"

"I'm sure he'll comply. He's still in the doghouse with me over taking the photos and blackmailing men behind my back. What do you want to know?"

"One, does Chet Ponyweather have anonymous sex in bathrooms and areas around Central Park? Two, I want to know about George Sheffield's past gay sexual habits—the dirtier, the better. Third, who was John Bekkman's last lover and was the breakup messy?"

"That's it?"

"That's it, Robert."

"So you're going to solve this whole matter out of the answers to those questions?"

"No, but it's a start."

* * *

I called Michael from my apartment and asked him to get some answers right away. He was only too eager to comply since this was the first time I had talked to him since our Death March across lower Manhattan.

"So what are you going to do now, Monette?"

"I'm going back to Brooklyn right now. I want to look over the photos on that CD for a while."

"I know. You're going to look and see if George Sheffield is wearing a Nazi SS ring or something," I said, trying to test my sinister organization theme.

"No, Robert. I don't think George is some escaped Nazi, although that would explain his behavior in dealing with some of his tenants."

"So what do you want me to do in the meantime, Monette?"

"Why don't you go back to your . . . I mean Michael's apartment and just do nothing."

"Actually, I was thinking about cleaning up my apartment. Just about anyone who's wanted to break into my apartment has already done so—I guess I'm safe for the time being."

"Yes, that might be a good idea. Actually, why don't you call Detective McMillan and see if he can tell you anything that might help us."

Monette left, and as I began to put things right, I called McMillan and tried to get something out of him. He answered on his cell phone.

"Robert, good to hear from you. Yes, after questioning Chet, it seems that he's scared shitless about his wife finding out about his dealings with Cody. Not only does he have a hostile partner who's trying to take over the import business he runs, but get this: His wife threatened to divorce him if she finds out he's been having sex behind her back again."

"Again? You mean he's done this before?"

"Over and over again, apparently."

I thought about Monette's question for Michael to re-search: Does Chet have anonymous sex in public places? *Touché*, Monette. I then thought of a question on my own.

"So far as we know, the only person who paid off Eric Bogert was John Bekkman, correct?"

"That is correct."

"How do you know that?"

"Because he showed me his bank statement. Plus, we got a court order and examined Eric's bank statements as well. There's a withdrawal from Mr. Bekkman's for forty thou-sand dollars and a deposit the next day in Eric's for the same amount."

Another thought sprang to my mind.

"But wasn't that rather stupid of Eric? I mean, depositing the money, that I assume was in cash. It leaves a paper trail."

"Robert, in all my years on the force, I have seen very few criminals that were really cunning. The really smart ones never get caught. But the bulk of them haven't made good plans, or they slip up somewhere along the line and do some-thing stupid. Some are just plain dumb. Eric was no master-mind."

"I gathered that."

"Robert, I have something to ask you," McMillan said.

The hairs on the back of my neck stood up. From the poignant, soft sound in his voice, I could tell what it was going to be.

"Robert, would you go out on a date with me tonight?"

Even though I had anticipated his question, I was still shocked. Shocked that someone else was interested in me, and shocked that McMillan was still pursuing me even though he knew that I already had a boyfriend, albeit a long-distance one.

"Um, gosh. I, I . . ." I stammered, trying to think fast. Did I want to jeopardize my present relationship with one of the best men I have ever met in order to perhaps have some fun? The funny thing was, I wasn't bowled over by McMillan. I began to suspect that my fascination in him was that he seemed fascinated with me. It was a new feeling and I liked it. Perhaps, besides the sex, this was what really lit Michael's fire—the knowledge that someone wanted him, if however short the duration.

"On one condition," I relented.

"Whatever you want, Robert."

"That we keep this strictly a date and no hot-and-heavy. Not right now."

"You got a deal."

I wish he hadn't put it quite like that. My guilt was already having me feel like a two-timing whore. But hadn't Marc told me to go out and explore, to live, as Auntie Mame said in the movie? The problem was, he didn't exactly say how far I should explore. But I put it down to the fact that, by nature, men were beasts, the operative word being *beasts*. I just wanted to explore my sadly underexplored beast side.

"I'll pick you up at Michael's at eight o'clock."

I hung up and decided not to call Marc on this one. Already, I was traveling down the road to perdition. No, I think I was skipping.

I told Monette what had happened—or was going to happen—with McMillan, and she took the only position that a good friend could take under the circumstances: as neutral as Switzerland.

"I'm sure you'll do the right thing, Robert," she said.

"But that's what I'm afraid of, Monette. The right thing

would be to stay home and watch reruns of *Ab Fab* while even people in Bangladesh go out and have a good time. But I'm tired of always doing the right thing. Look where it's gotten me."

"I think you just told yourself what to do—you're just not listening."

"You mean that you think I should go out?"

"No, not what *I* think you should do . . . but what *you* want to do. You know what your heart is telling you to do."

"It's not my heart that I'm worrying about. I'm confused whether I'm listening to my heart or whether my penis is doing all the talking."

"So what if you listen to your penis once in a while? You're only human."

"Do you ever listen to your vagina, Monette?"

"Yes, all the time, Robert."

"And what does it say?"

"It says for me to get a date because if there isn't some action down there soon, my parts will freeze up from lack of use."

"So if I go out on this date, you won't think of me as an amoralistic whore?"

"Listen, you will never become a whore, amoralistic or otherwise—it's not in you."

"So what's on your plate tonight, Monette?"

"I'm going to go through the CD of photos tonight, watch reruns of *Ab Fab*, then go to bed."

"I think I've just made up my mind about tonight."

"Go, have a good time," Monette said, blessing me in the process. "Just remember that asking to wear his handcuffs on the first date is considered a little forward."

19

I'm Getting Closer, I Can Feel It

That night, the amoralistic whore went two-timing and had a great time. We had dinner, then went for drinks at a jazz club. We talked the whole night about everything except murders, bodybuilders, and photo CDs.

When the time came to say good night and he pulled up in front of Michael's building, there was that inevitable, uncomfortable moment where the two of us stared through the windshield and into space, waiting for one of us to make the first move. McMillan, as I expected, made it.

As tenderly as an infant surgeon, he held my chin in his hand and slowly turned my head to face his. He closed his eyes and pulled my lips toward his, violating our earlier agreement to keep the night platonic. I felt trapped, enjoying the carnal spark that ignited between us, but at the same time felt that I was being disloyal and dishonest to Marc. What to do, what to do?

Just as his lips met mine, I farted.

Not a tiny squeaker fart with a slow release in a high-pitched whine that continues higher until it runs out of steam or floats higher than human ears can detect. No, this was a huge, loud, voluminous fart, a B-R-A-A-A-T of a fart that almost shattered the windows of the car, or at least required that they be opened for a few minutes. Freud would have said I did it purposely, to avoid an uncomfortable situation. Maybe I did, but to this very day (where it still haunts me), I maintain that the romantic gravity of the situation made me hold my breath and the lentil soup consumed hours before at dinner did the rest.

The night ended with a few chuckles, followed by a hug and a smile. Luke drove off (with the windows still open) slowly into the night. I had remained true to Marc—for now.

When I got to the apartment, Michael wasn't there, which didn't surprise me. Since he had run through most of the men in Manhattan (and several other acceptable boroughs of New York), weekends provided an influx of new meat on which Michael could pounce—and pounce he did like Winona Ryder on an unguarded exit door in a Saks Fifth Avenue dress department.

With the apartment all to myself, I had a good long soak in Michael's spa then went to bed.

I dreamed of Africa, the Spanish Inquisition being conducted by mice, then of a ski-masked man holding a white cloth in one hand and a bottle in the other. There was a strange, sweet medicine smell in the air. I had only begun to think, what a strange dream this is, when I got the shock of my life: It was no dream. There was a real, live murderer standing only a few inches away from me. The adrenaline hit me like a bucket of scalding hot water, every muscle in my body ready to spring like a cat. In a millisecond, I deduced that the assailant didn't know I was awake since I hadn't yet moved, and anyway I was frozen with fear. It's funny how, at moments like this, you can spend what seems like hours assessing the situation and deciding on a course of action—when in reality, only a few seconds pass. But the decision had been made—I had the element of surprise on my side and I acted on it.

My foot flew up at my attacker's groin and connected with a strong thud, sending the thug into a bent-over position. He wobbled back and forth like a drunk on roller skates, then fell to the floor and was strangely silent.

Had I killed him?

I sprang up to turn on the light and found the goon out cold. I reached down to pick up the bottle that had spilled on his chest and was hit by a wave of dizziness. It must be chloroform. I grabbed a T-shirt and covered my nose and mouth with it to avoid any more of the noxious fumes and I carefully righted the bottle without adding my fingerprints to the surface. My kick had caused the assailant to spill enough of the fluid on his chest and neck to knock him out. But for how long? Not having been chloroformed in my life, I didn't know how long it would work, so I ran down the hall to get Michael to help me in tying the guy up.

I burst into Michael's room and yelled for him to get up, but there was no response. I turned on the light and found Michael in bed with some guy I couldn't possibly bring home even with a fist full of gold. Both were out cold, but at least I could hear them breathing. I tried to shake Michael awake, but to no avail. Our attacker must have chloroformed Michael and his trick first, then came to finish me off . . . *Finish me off.* The realization sent a chill right down my spine. If I didn't wake up when I did, I would probably be kissing the pavement in front of Michael's building, with Michael and his date splattering nearby. I started shaking uncontrollably, my own mortality staring me right in the face. Sure, I had been threatened with death before, but it had always been obliquely wielded, funneled through notes or phone calls, never approaching me in the flesh and blood. There was, however, no time to waste.

I ran into Michael's closet to get some belts to secure my prisoner, but found that Michael's kinky sexual nature came in even handier: Michael had all sorts of handcuffs and leather restraints that he used with certain guys, so I grabbed a handful of them and headed back to my bedroom.

I took the restraints and tied up our assailant so securely that I wasn't even sure the police would be able to undo him after they arrived. Then I unmasked our visitor, expecting to see a familiar face. Nope. I didn't recognize him and couldn't even tell if he was one of the two men who chased Eric out of the gym that fateful day. I called McMillan, who was sound asleep at his house in White Plains, then dialed 911. Before Michael even came to, his apartment was crawling with police and paramedics. In fact, when he came out of his chloroform haze and saw all the uniformed men moving in and out of the room, he asked if he was in Heaven.

"No, Michael, not quite. But we were about this far," I said, gesturing with my finger and thumb, "from ending up there."

"No kidding!" he exclaimed. "You saved my life again, Robert!"

It was true. For the second time, I had saved his life. This coup would at least guarantee me several weeks' stay this summer at his house on Fire Island.

"Oh, Michael, did you find out the answers to the questions I gave you?"

"Yes. Chet Ponyweather is a regular fixture to the Brambles in Central Park. In fact, Tom Rochambeau, a friend of mine, is a regular there, too. Chet was there for almost two hours on the night Eric was pushed to his death, servicing Tom's member."

"So that's where he was!" I said, another ray of light shining on my understanding of what was really going on.

"Question two. George Sheffield. He's been a big baby

for a long time now. Over ten years, according to guys I've talked to. Jahn, a furniture designer who is big, big, big now, built an oversize crib for Sheffield years ago. His chauffeur ordered it and paid for it, but Jahn said he recognized the delivery address because he went to a dinner at a gay couple's apartment right across the hall. And as for John Bekkman, yes, his breakup with his last lover, Drake, was very messy. I think, as my sources tell me, Drake poured a tureen of curry carrot soup over John's head at Le Cirque three years ago. At least I think it was curry carrot, or maybe it was sweet potato soup with curry. Oh, yes, then he force-fed John a napkin."

"And do you have the address and phone number of this ex of John's?"

"Yes I do," Michael said, handing me a slip of paper.

Michael was all too happy to oblige me, seeing that he owed his life to me—again. It wouldn't last long because the afterglow would soon be gone and Michael would conveniently forget. The key was to extract as many concessions and favors as you could before the bloom fell off the rose.

Since McMillan would take at least an hour or more to arrive, another policeman questioned me about what had happened. From his investigation, I could ascertain what they had found concerning our attacker. The alarm system had been tampered with—which didn't matter anyway, since it had not been turned on. The elevator key control had been easily jumped with a plain copper wire. Our assailant had climbed out of a window in the hall and had swung on a rope halfway around the building to reach the apartment's balcony, entering through a patio door that was unlocked. And the only thing that had fingerprints all over it was the ass belonging to Michael's date.

When I relayed this information to Monette the next morning over the phone, she was astounded.

"Well, it looks like the police have their hands on part of the team who murdered Cody and Eric. I guess they're not completely incompetent."

"You think they've been messy?"

"Robert, what I'm going to say about Luke McMillan the detective isn't how I might feel about McMillan the person, but it seems like he's missed some obvious clues."

"You mean like missing the entry point on the window in my apartment?"

"Yes, that was one clue."

"What others?"

"He never investigated how the window latch got secured again once the intruder had left."

"Are these points really that important, Monette? It seems like there are so many more bigger things—like who was driving those cars that tried to run me down."

"The littlest clues often end up being the most important, Robert. How long has McMillan been a homicide detective?"

"I don't know, Monette. A few years. He said something about working for another division before that."

"He didn't say what, did he? It wasn't the parking violation bureau, was it?"

"No, he wasn't a meter maid, Monette. It was some special division."

"Could you find out? We might need to confide in someone in his department who is more on the ball—a superior maybe. I want you to keep your romantic dalliances separate from the job he's doing. This is your life we're talking about—you've got to have a clear head about this."

"That makes total sense. But I don't want to do an end run around McMillan and have him find out later."

"Don't worry . . . he won't hear a thing about it."

"So what's our next step, Monette?"

"I think we should pay a short visit to John Bekkman's ex. I have to rule out something there. Let me give him a call and I'll call you back."

"Right, bye," I said and hung up the phone.

Michael, who had actually given his bedmate breakfast, was now standing at my side, waiting to tell me something important.

"Yes, Michael, what is it?"

"Could you tell my trick that last night wasn't planned? He thinks the whole chloroform, ski-masked-attacker thing was on purpose and the whole episode is giving him a raging hard-on. Please help me."

"I think I have a man who is perfect for him. Just ask your trick if he minds riding in the trunk of a car."

20

How to Curry Favor from an Ex-Boyfriend

A few hours later, we met John Bekkman's ex at a restaurant for brunch, with us agreeing to pick up the tab. One glance at Drake Hobart left no doubt as to why a romance between him and John was doomed from the very beginning. Whereas John was outdoorsy and dynamic, Drake was the epitome of a forty-plus New York City queen. From the yellow cable-knit cotton sweater thrown lightly over his shoulders to the feminine slipper-like shoes that graced his feet (not to mention his dyed yellow hair that was way too long for the first decade of the new millennium), Drake probably broke out in hives over the thought of ever having to leave the isle of Manhattan. Whatever brought them together in the first place would remain as elusive as what came seconds before the universe's Big Bang.

"So you dumped a tureen of soup on his head?" Monette asked with a chuckle.

"The whole thing, right there in his seat with everyone watching," Drake stated proudly. "The son of a bitch just dumped me after seven years. Seven years!"

"Seven years!" I exclaimed. "Is that diamonds? Or is it paper?"

Monette jumped in. "No, I think that anyone who can stay together for seven years deserves real estate, like an island. Capri maybe."

"Well, he deserved far worse than that for dumping me for Mr. Muscles."

I shook my head in disgust. "Isn't that always the way! You have him rolling in the aisles with your wit, you cook like Wolfgang Puck, you subvert your needs to his, and some musclehead catches his eyes with washboard abs and your boyfriend dumps you like Donna Summer dumped her gay fans when she went Christian."

"Ain't it the truth!" Drake lamented. "I said, 'John, you're dumping me for a guy who works for the circus?'"

Monette and I eyed each other in amazement as if we had just discovered the mother lode. Indeed, we had.

Monette shuddered briefly, then forged ahead.

"The circus, you say? Like Ringling Brothers?"

"No, no. Cirque de Soleil."

Another flash of discovery between the two of us.

"Drake, could you tell us what role he had in Cirque?" Monette said, beaming like she was on the cusp of a great discovery.

"He was a contortionist. You see, he was Asian and had a very small frame. He was, like five-feet-four or something like that. He could climb up poles with just his hands, pulling his body up without even using his feet. And he could fit inside tiny boxes they used in the act, which is unusual for a man since women are usually contortionists. It has something to do with the way the female body is constructed."

Monette was frothing over with excitement. I wasn't as hot on the trail as she was, but I could sense the general direction her logic was taking her.

"Drake," she continued, "do you know if John is still with this guy?"

"His name's Michael. Michael Lau. Yes, I'm sure he is. You don't see a lot of them together. Michael stays in the background because he was fired from Cirque for not showing up for work . . . he trained and trained with the circus, then turned into a big no-show. I guess once he became boyfriends with John, he no longer had to work. John, if you didn't know it, is stinking rich."

"We did some research on John," I added. "He's quite the adventurer, isn't he?"

"That was part of what put the final nail in the coffin of our relationship—besides Michael Lau, that is."

"And how was that?" Monette inquired.

"Oh God, he was always off with his buddies, white-water rafting some river in Chile, kayaking some lake in Argentina, spelunking some cave in Hawaii," Drake reported.

"And you didn't want to join him on his outings, if you don't mind me asking?"

"No, Robert, I could care less about John or being outdoors. It didn't matter anyway since he dissuaded me from accompanying him and his buddies."

"His buddies?" Monette asked in surprise.

"Oh, like I was cuckolded or something? No, I don't ever think he had sex with these guys, although I wouldn't blame him if he did."

"Why was that?" I asked.

"Oh, they were ex-cops, mountaineers, real athletic guys."

"I see," Monette said through a haze of deep thought. "Drake, I have one last question for you, and I need an accurate answer, so think very carefully and if you're not sure, call me back when you have the answer."

Drake looked amused, as if the answer to a single, simple question would be so earth-shaking.

"Yeah, go ahead," he answered with a slightly nervous chuckle.

"Where was John on December seventh, 2002?"

"Oh, that's easy. We were in Amsterdam for our anniversary . . . an anniversary I will never forget—our last."

"And why is that?" Monette asked.

"Because he got me drunk and I slept the whole night. Then after we got back to the States a week later, he broke up with me. Some anniversary, huh?"

Monette shook her head in sympathy. "Yeah, some anniversary."

We finished our lunch hurriedly, paid the bill, and thanked Drake graciously over and over. Monette grabbed my arm and dragged me to the street curb, furiously flagged down a cab, and pulled me inside.

"We've got work to do," she said breathlessly, as if there wasn't a moment to lose. "We'll go to Michael's apartment and I'll spill everything. Then we need to call McMillan and tell him everything."

I sat staring out at the buildings rushing by while Monette bit her lip and tapped her hand nervously on the cab's window ledge. We arrived at Michael's apartment, walked right past the sleeping doorman, and were whisked up the elevator, where Monette practically tugged me down the hall and broke down Michael's apartment door in excitement.

"We need to look at the CD again. Let's go down to the computer room!" she said, barging through the door and surprising a naked Michael in mid-jerk, webcamming with another naked guy on the plasma screen in front of him.

"Michael, could you leave us, please! This is an emergency!" she said, pushing him out the door of his own room and throwing a T-shirt at him that he'd left behind in the rush, inscribed with the caption, IF I WANT YOUR OPINION, I'LL TAKE MY DICK OUT OF YOUR MOUTH AND ASK YOU.

I could hear Michael grab something out of a hall closet, followed by a loud slam of his apartment door, indicating he had gone out in a rage.

Monette was on a mission. Her fingers pecked on the keyboard like a frantic chicken and brought up the infamous photo CD.

"So I suppose you're going to tell me what this is all about?"

"All in good time, my pretty, all in good time," she shot out of the corner of her mouth as she tapped away.

"There! See!"

"Yeah, it's a picture of John Bekkman having a fantasy in the living room of his apartment. I don't see what's so important about it."

"Remember what you said about some sinister organization in the background?"

"Yes," I said, peering at the photo. "I don't see anything in the background that looks sinister." I squinted at the walls and furniture, trying like the dickens to see a hidden swastika, hammer and sickle, or even a freemason's logo. "All I see are a bunch of paintings."

Monette put her finger on her nose while pointing another at me; her sign for "on the nose, buddy boy."

"Whaaat?!" I stammered. "The guy collects art and donates it to museums. I don't see what's so special about that."

"That painting you see there on the wall," she said, pointing to a Van Gogh, "was one of two pictures stolen from the Van Gogh Museum in Amsterdam during the early morning hours on December seventh, 2002."

My mouth opened but no sound came out of it. I remained silent while the enormity of the thought sank in.

"OH SHIT!" I eventually managed to eke out.

"Oh shit is right," Monette said, the tone in her voice echoing the heavy atmosphere that descended over the room. We were up against a conspiracy that involved dollars that made Eric's pitiful blackmail scheme look like eating a few grapes at the local Safeway without paying for them.

"But I didn't see the painting when we visited John . . . come to think of it," I said.

"You're right. Neither did I—at first. Remember when I commented that the wall had been painted recently because it smelled of paint. In the photo here, the wall behind the painting is a vivid yellow, like in Van Gogh's masterpiece. But when he put up a Kandinsky in its place, he had the wall painted red to show the work off to its best."

The light was dawning on me finally.

"So when John had Cody photograph him in a sexual scene in his apartment, he was probably so in the heat of passion that he forgot about the painting. Plus, he was blindfolded at the time, so he wasn't thinking. Afterwards, he either realized that he had made a big mistake or Eric gave him a sample of the photos—it doesn't matter since the cat was just about out of the bag. The thing was, if John were able to contain the number of people who viewed the CD, he had the hope that no one would notice the stolen artwork on his walls. And to be truthful, few people would."

"I got you so far, Monette, but what made you start thinking that John was our man?"

"Robert, it was so simple. Someone went to a lot of trouble to get into your apartment. Clue one: a very elaborate break-in. Clue number two: Once we discovered that someone shimmied down between two walls—probably to keep the number of burglars to a minimum because of the reporters—I suspected that John was involved. After all, John was an adventurer, he had a taste for dangerous sports, like kayaking, skydiving, and—"

"Mountain climbing," I said, finishing Monette's thought. "Of course, how could I have been so stupid?!"

"You see what I meant about the little clues being important. If you examined *how* someone broke into your apartment, it could tell you far more than *why* they did it."

"Okay, here's something that's been bugging me: How did my idea of a sinister organization get you thinking about John? Did my comment get you thinking about a ring of art thieves?"

"No, it wasn't that at all. The only word that made me think of looking at the pictures more intensely wasn't your idea of *a sinister organization in the background*—just the word *background*. You see, I know the blackmailees had a lot at stake, but not enough to kill two people and set their target on a third, fourth, and maybe more. I felt that there was something we couldn't see in the photos that merited going on a killing spree, so I sat down and started looking at everything item by item, what was in the room, what was visible outside windows, what people were wearing, who was doing what, and when I saw the artwork in various apartments, I started thinking. Was some of it stolen? Was some of it forged? So I looked up each piece on the Internet, and before long, eureka!"

"Well, I, for one, think we should get on the phone to McMillan and let him know we've cracked the case."

"My sentiments exactly," Monette echoed.

"You talk to him, Monette, since you figured everything out."

So we got McMillan on the phone and Monette gave a breathless account of how she'd unraveled the case of the Flying Personal Trainers. McMillan asked all kinds of questions: How did we find out about John Bekkman's ex-boyfriend, how did we know of John's whereabouts the day of the break-in at the Van Gogh Museum, and how did we figure out how John or an accomplice entered Robert's apartment without leaving any traces?

McMillan must have complimented Monette and I one hundred times, because Monette kept saying "thank you" or "we're flattered" or "it wasn't anything two insanely intelligent geniuses couldn't do."

"Yes, well, thank you, Detective. I think that we'd be flattered and glad to have a celebratory dinner," Monette said into the phone. "Champagne, oh, Robert and I have never had enough, but I'm warning you," she laughed, "you'd better get our statements *before* we have that magnum of champagne! Okay, fine, Robert and I aren't doing anything else the rest of the day. Great, see you downstairs in one hour."

Monette hung up the phone and was absolutely glowing.

"So I take it he wants us to make some statements at the station, then he's taking us out to dinner?"

"You got it. He said he's a little embarrassed that he missed such obvious clues, but I told him that we wouldn't tell his department that we solved the case since it would probably mean a promotion. He's going to be indebted to you for this, Robert."

"That's what I'm worried about."

"What do you mean?"

"It complicates the situation, Monette."

"What, are you having feelings about McMillan?"

"I don't know. I can't seem to separate whether I'm interested in him because he's interested in me, or whether it's the real thing. Marc is still very much in the picture, Monette. It was just so much easier when I only had one guy to worry about. Now I've got two to choose between."

"Robert, I would kill to be in your position. The only

thing I have to choose between is my vibrators. Hmm, the Tornado or Earth Mover?" she said, weighing the afore-mentioned devices in her hands like scales of pleasure. "Robert, I have tried to stay out of your situation because I'm sure you will make the right decision, but I will give you one piece of advice."

"And that is?"

"Just let things play out. Sometimes, you don't have to make the decision—the decision is often made for you. Just give it time and enjoy yourself. Remember, life is not a dress rehearsal."

I walked up to her and gave her a hug that lasted a long, long time. Just then, we heard Michael's key in the door. Being mechanically inept, it took Michael close to a minute of struggling, rattling of keys, followed by a volley of cussing before he was able to open the two locks protecting him from the outside world.

Monette released her hug on me, then quickly relayed a few words of caution from McMillan. "He asked us not to tell anyone about solving the case just yet. He's got to get a court order to put a wiretap on Bekkman—he wants to get the whole gang in one fell swoop. So not a word to anyone, especially big-mouth Michael."

"I promise, Monette."

"One other thing, Robert. I wasn't going to tell you this, but McMillan said he had an important question to ask you tonight."

Marriage. I knew it! He was going to force me into a de-cision tonight.

"Are you two finished looking at your dirty pictures?" Michael said when he entered his apartment, taking off his expensive leather jacket and heaving it across the room in a high arc. It landed carelessly on the floor, a crumpled piece of two-thousand-dollar animal hide that would be given away the moment the new fall collections of menswear hit the racks at Barney's.

"Yes, we're finished. We're going out to dinner tonight with Detective McMillan to discuss the details of the case," I blurted out, trying to make our night sound as boring as I could. I didn't want Michael tagging along on this, of all nights. "Just routine stuff."

"Sounds *fascinating*," Michael said sarcastically.

"Michael, I would think that dinner with a *real* cop would be something you would dive at," I slid in.

"See, that's the thing that separates you from me, Robert. I wouldn't waste time with dinner. I'd get him in the sack right away, and I'd tell him to bring his gun, leave his leather search gloves on, and we could spend the evening doing some cavity searches. Now, if you'll excuse me, I have to go get ready for my date," Michael said as he sauntered down the hall to his bedroom, George Clooney, Bluebeard the Pirate, and Mae West all rolled into one.

"That's Michael for you," I remarked to Monette. "A Ruger .357 magnum in his pants and it's always loaded."

We had a drink, talked a little, then got our coats on to go out to dinner.

"Wait," Michael said, appearing out of nowhere. "I'll ride down with you two."

We made Michael turn on the alarm and lock both locks, then we got into the elevator and descended down to the lobby, where the doorman was reading a magazine, barely looking up to see us leave the building. We could've been carrying out a television set and a stereo and rolling a rack of fur coats and leather jackets and the doorman wouldn't have noticed a thing.

McMillan was waiting at the curb for Monette and me. Michael was going to take off on his *date* without even acknowledging the detective, but I grabbed hold of his jacket and at least made him say hi to Luke.

"Michael Stark, this is Luke McMillan," I said proudly.

"Nice to meet you, Detective . . . hey, I remember you . . . from a long time ago."

"I don't see when," McMillan said through the open passenger-side window.

"Yes, we met before!" Michael said adamantly.

Shit, shit, shit, shit, shit. It was too good to be true. Here is a man who's madly in love with me and I find out the night he's going to pop the question that Michael has already slept with him.

"No, remember when that fucking creep-of-a-boyfriend of mine stole my Matisse and made off with it? You came to my apartment and snooped around, remember?"

I was somewhat relieved, but it still didn't mean that Michael hadn't porked the guy.

"Michael," I said, suddenly remembering the details of that incident, "that wasn't McMillan. The detective's name was Rickles."

Michael, who couldn't remember a man's name five minutes after he'd had his way with him, kept on, determined to wreck my budding relationship with Luke.

"I wasn't talking about Rickles. I remember you were a cop working under Rickles in that special forces department that deals with artworks theft."

"I don't remember that, Michael. I handle over two hundred cases a year. It's all a haze in my head."

"I'm sure it was you!" Michael continued. "I tried to cruise you, but you weren't interested because you were trying to do your job. Such a shame. All work and no play . . ." Michael trailed off, cruising my potential new boyfriend right in front of my face. It wouldn't be the first time.

"Uh, Michael, we've got to go now. Have fun on your date!" I said, pushing Michael down the sidewalk and away from the car.

"And you have fun on yours," Michael responded, the words slithering out of his mouth and snaking up the detective's pant leg.

"Sorry," I apologized to McMillan as we got into the squad car, me getting in the front and Monette into the back. "Michael will come on to anyone," I said, dealing McMillan an unintentional insult. "I, I didn't mean it the way it came out."

McMillan laughed, pushing his metal clipboard notebook aside so I could sit closer to him. The damn thing was so big, I couldn't fit it on the other side of me, so I held it in my lap, caressing the official equipment in my sweaty hands. He eased the car into traffic and pointed the car in the direction of his offices downtown.

"Don't worry about Michael, Robert," he said. "I get cruised by all kinds of people in my job. Men, women, even teenage daughters. It must be the badge or something. Or the uniform."

"But you don't wear a uniform anymore," I replied. "Although I would like to see you in one . . . someday."

"Robert, I'll pull it out and put it on just for you," he said, laying a hand on my leg.

His hand made my leg warm where he touched me. His touch also caused another reaction, but I won't go into that for now. You get the idea. Since Monette was in the backseat, I didn't want things to get smutty in front of her. She was very silent, so I tried to get her involved in the conversation. I turned around and spoke to her through the wire grid that separated me from her.

"You look like a criminal back there, Monette," I joked.

"Don't joke. This isn't my first time in the backseat of one of these," she admitted.

"Monette! You were arrested once? You never told me that!"

"It happened before I knew you, Robert. I was protesting the building of some tract home development on a frog breeding ground."

"My, you are the ecological one, aren't you?" I commented. "Who won?"

"The same one who always does. The developer," she lamented with a sigh. "They ended up bulldozing the sight in the middle of the night and the fuck got away with it because money talks. The frogs got revenge in the end, however."

"And how was that?" McMillan asked.

"It turns out that the ground was filled with hidden underground springs that didn't show up on surveys and the whole development was unstable. All the house foundations cracked, and the houses they were able to build had to be abandoned. The whole thing is still in court and the developer went bankrupt. The end . . . maybe. Detective?"

"Yes?"

"There's one fact about this case that bothers me," Monette said.

"Yes?"

"You said that John Bekkman had an airtight alibi?"

"Yes, but criminals can lie."

"I guess he did," Monette replied.

"So how did he establish an alibi?" I asked. "Did he get friends to lie for him?"

"Yes, one of his cohorts, Marshall Bryne, said he was with them hiking out of town. He's under surveillance as we speak and we're getting a court order to have his phone tapped. We need more than just circumstantial evidence for a strong case."

"Excellent," Monette agreed. "As for the bank statement that Bekkman showed you . . . the one that showed a payment to Eric Bogert?"

"The one for sixty thousand?"

"Yes, that one," Monette said. "I suppose that was a fake?"

"Oh sure. It doesn't take much to create a fake bank statement nowadays. Anyone with a computer can create a reasonable facsimile. But remember, Monette, this guy was slick and the statement he showed me looked like the real thing. The guy has money. I'm sure he had someone make it up for him."

"You're right. I should have seen right through that one," Monette replied.

"Wait a minute," I spoke up. "Luke, you just said the payment was for sixty thousand. The other day, you said it was for forty thousand. But John Bekkman told us that he paid Eric fifty thousand dollars."

"Did I?" McMillan said, shaking his head. "I goofed on that one . . . I guess I've been working too hard. See what happens when you call me day and night?" He laughed.

"I guess you have been working too hard, Luke. The station is in the other direction," I pointed out. I was about to tell him how turned around he was when I found myself staring into the barrel of a gun.

"That's right," Monette said from the backseat. "Our friend here is in cahoots with John Bekkman."

I was going to say something stupid such as "NO, LUKE, NOT YOU!" but felt that the pistol pointed in my direction made that all unnecessary. Monette was being rather calm about what was happening, but I imagined that the door handles in the backseat of the police cruiser didn't work, so there was little she could do. Unfortunately, it was all up to me. I started thinking desperately of a way to save us, but short of me zooming out of the front seat with the help of a rocket belt hidden underneath my clothing, I didn't see a lot of alternatives.

Monette broke the tension in the car.

"I had some suspicions that you might have been involved," she said.

"And what tipped you off?" he replied.

"The first thing was that you could be so sloppy in your investigations. If you weren't deliberately overlooking clues, then you were covering them up."

"Covering up?" McMillan said, taking a hard turn and heading in the direction of the docks on Manhattan's Lower East Side. I noticed that even though he was driving a tad rapidly, his gun stayed trained on me the whole time.

"Everyone missed it, but the window latch in Robert's apartment gave you away," she said smugly. "Robert and I discovered how the window was drilled and pushed open, but closing it wasn't so easy. Robert swore up and down that he had latched the window before he left that day, and if you know obsessive-compulsive Robert like I know him, he locked that window that day."

"So what does that mean?" McMillan said with a knowing chuckle.

"The window was latched after the burglary, meaning you went up first and, while the investigation was going on, went over to the window and latched it yourself to take the focus away from the window as an entry point."

"You are clever, Monette."

"But why wreck Robert's place after the burglary? To scare him?"

"You tell me," came the reply.

"You were also the person who cut the lock on Robert's locker at Club M and removed the original CD-ROM before Robert had a chance to give it to you. I think you were already there at the gym, waiting for Robert to arrive, knowing that if you weren't there yet, Robert would lock his gym bag containing the CD in a locker. When Robert was on the treadmill, you slipped into the locker room, cut the lock, got your hands on the CD, and then made a big show of arriving to make Robert think you had just gotten there."

"That's what you think, huh?" McMillan said, remaining cagey to avoid spilling any information. The guy was going to shoot us soon probably in some warehouse in lower Manhattan, but he was still hedging his bets.

"I also surmised that you called the reporters and told them that Robert had the CD so that all the other suspects would know where Robert lived. You then waited for some of them to do what you knew they would: try and break into Robert's apartment so that you could start implicating them as having murdered Cody Walker and Eric Bogert."

"An interesting theory," McMillan conceded.

I wasn't sure whether Monette was deliberately trying to bait McMillan for some purpose to make him nervous, but to what purpose? Or was she just trying to show that the clues he had left would eventually be discovered by another investigator. In any case, I felt it was a long shot and would do us no good when we had bullets in our heads.

Strangely enough, McMillan cracked enough to let us know our fates.

"You would have made a good detective, Monette. Would have, I said, because that won't help you once Chet Ponyweather shoots the two of you."

I was stunned. Monette was stunned.

"He's waiting for us to arrive at a warehouse."

There was an uncomfortable silence in the car for far too long. I was still trying to find a way out of this mess, but the wheels in Monette's head were still turning.

"Ah," came the voice in triumph from the confines of the backseat. "Let me guess. Chet Ponyweather smuggled the Van Goghs out of the Netherlands for you via his shipping firm and he's wrapped up in all of this. He's waiting there for us to arrive and you are going to shoot him, then make it look like he shot the two of us and you'll make it look like he killed us to keep the CD photos quiet and save his marriage and his company. And his role in smuggling the Van Goghs out of the Netherlands dies with him. Am I right?" Monette asked.

"You are correct," McMillan said, finally giving in a bit. "Not that your knowledge is going to do you any good."

They say that at times like these, your whole life flashes in front of you, and I want to go on record and tell you that this is a big crock of shit. The only thing that flashed through my mind was why a car company would plaster a warning label about baby seats and airbags on the sun visor of a car where you couldn't read the yellow and red warning unless you had the visor down in your face. I guessed that they were just trying to avoid another lawsuit from a stupid parent who would inadvertently turn her child seat into a projectile . . .

In the wink of an eye, I grabbed McMillan's arm and smashed his hand against the windshield. With my free right hand, I grabbed the steering wheel of the car and jerked it to the far right while stomping on the gas pedal at the same time. Being a police cruiser with an oversize engine in it, the car lifted off the pavement and flew into the stratosphere while I tossed McMillan's metal clipboard in front of the steering wheel. A millisecond later, the airbag inflated, followed by a huge bang and the sound of breaking glass and metal being twisted and crushed. Then everything went black—a deeper black than I have ever experienced.

21

If This Is Heaven, Then Why Does It Smell Like Urine?

To make matters short, I was dead. Monette was dead. McMillan was dead. The whole world was dead. So why was I strapped to a board and being lifted into an ambulance? Couldn't Heaven get its shit together? And why were there paramedics in Heaven? What a farce! I thought there was no sickness, no pain. So why did my ribs hurt so much? And my hip? Why were such thoughts going through my head?

It was all a great, big lie. Sister Mary O'Grady had lied to us in third grade catechism. Heaven wasn't a great big city full of light and angels singing wondrous hymns. It smelled like urine and dog poop and garbage dumpster drippings mixed with cigarette butts. Some afterlife, I thought. You try to be good and get some reward in the Great Beyond and it turns out to resemble New York on a late spring night. The ultimate screw job! Then everything went black again.

When my eyes opened again, Marc Baldwin was looking down at me. Well, all right, I thought. Finally, something is going my way. Maybe Heaven is okay after all. You get to be with the one you love and get to have endless sex and long, protracted lunches at the Union Square Café and get to sit at the coveted main room tables having mouth-watering pasta dishes that taste so good they could make you cry, followed by dessert with glasses of grappa and tiny demitasse cups of espresso. I was beginning to like this. Even better, I wouldn't have to live in a crappy, substandard apartment and work in advertising writing brochures and sampler package copy for feminine hygiene products that make vaginas smell like fresh papayas.

"Robert?" came a voice on high. "Robert?"

God was calling my name. I was an avowed agnostic, but God was calling my name.

"Robert?" He injected himself into my dream again. No wonder people said this guy was omnipresent—you couldn't even have any peace in your dreams. Why was he bothering me again?

"Robert? It's Marc! Are you there?"

Again with the pestering. Didn't God know not to pester people? If he could read people's minds, didn't he get it that I wanted to be left alone with my dreams?

"Robert? It's me, Buddha."

Oh fuck, now I was in trouble! I spend all this time being indoctrinated by Sister Mary O'Grady and now it turns out that I got an even bigger screw: God is a Buddhist. What could you expect from a nun I had caught drinking holy water from a bottle in the coatroom in third grade catechism? At least that's what she told me was in the bottle. A few months later, in homage to Christ, she nailed her hands to the desk in her room at the convent, requiring three firemen and a physician to free her. Afterward, I heard she was transferred to a convent in Montana for some much-needed rest. I guess it was all that holy water—she got too holy for her own good, which would go a long way in explaining her holier-than-thou attitude. But I digress.

"Robert? It's Marc. Marc Baldwin. Remember me, your boyfriend, from Palm Springs. Er, Cathedral City, if you want to be technical."

This was not heaven, but something very close to it. I felt a hand grabbing mine and felt the warmth travel up my arm to my heart. It felt comforting and safe.

"Robert, there you are," the voice said. "You've been in a very bad accident, but the doctors said you're going to be okay. You've got three fractured ribs, and two hairline cracks in your pelvis, but you're going to be okay. You're on morphine now to ease the pain, so you're going to be a bit logy."

Suddenly, it started to rain. Not a big, summer thunder-storm drenching, but enough to splatter on the hood of your car and make you want to wash it—if you had one. Through the opium-den haze of the morphine, I could tell that Marc was crying, his tears falling on my arm and chest. I wanted to cry too, but all I could do was laugh like a drunk at a joke that wasn't funny to the sober.

"Monette is here and she wants to see you. Even Michael is here—imagine that—Michael is here!"

I felt two people come into the room and I immediately knew that I was not in Heaven, but in some place far bet-ter—I was surrounded by dear, dear friends.

I got out of the hospital in a few days, mostly because my shitty insurance plan wouldn't let me stay beyond seventy-two hours. I went to my temporary apartment in Michael's place. I didn't really want to stay there because living with Michael wasn't the best place for recuperation, owing to the constant comings and goings of tricks, but at least it had an elevator. The doctors agreed that my fifth-floor walk-up was too much for me to handle under the present circumstances, so I relented. It's amazing what eighty milligrams of Vicodin every six hours could do for your resolve to hang tough on your own. So I stayed at Michael's place for a while and heard my tale of bravery repeated over and over, but strangely enough, I never got tired of hearing it.

By now, you're probably wondering what happened to Luke McMillan, Chet Ponyweather, John Bekkman, Michael Lau, and the goons who chased Eric and Cody and probably helped break into the Van Gogh Museum. They were all behind bars now, awaiting the results of a grand jury investigation. I could see Luke now, his mangled nose hidden in a swath of bandages from the clipboard that I had sent flying into his face. Monette, who suffered a few facial bruises and a gash on her forehead, said my quick thinking had sent the cruiser crashing through a storefront window, setting off burglar alarms in three buildings at once. I had knocked McMillan out cold and Monette managed to kick out the broken back windows and get the gun out of the front seat. She said she stood on the sidewalk crying for help, then crying like a baby, wondering if I had given up the ghost.

I had a physical therapist who visited me daily for two weeks to help me get back on my feet, however unsteadily— then my insurance ran out. Bye-bye, therapist. But it was Marc who pushed me, got me to do my exercises every day, and helped me get out of and into bed, which was a Herculean effort in itself. And it was he and Michael who threw a party in my honor three weeks later, when I was able to get up and around with a cane, all by myself.

"My little hero," Monette said as she placed a kiss on my forehead. I was the king of the moment, sitting at the head of Michael's dining room table. There were several gifts on the table wrapped in wonderful handmade paper—a favorite of mine.

"Go on, open them," Marc urged. "Start with mine first."
I tore at the paper like a little kid on Christmas morning.
"A soccer ball . . . very funny!" I responded.

Marc was looking very satisfied with his gift. Or should I say smug.

"Open the next one—it's from me, too."

I proceeded to open it, but much more slowly. I had opened only one gift, but a theme of practical jokes seemed to be established by now and I could sense that Monette was directly behind it.

I opened the box and removed the contents. "An athletic supporter. How thoughtful," I said, feigning thankfulness.

"Wait, there's more," Marc informed me. "Look down at the bottom."

"Oh, Marc, you shouldn't have!" I said, lifting the protective crotch device worn by boxers out of the gift box. (I had to admit, it did look kinda sexy, but I didn't dare reveal this in front of everybody . . . I was still hearing jokes about wearing a saddle in Berlin to this very day. With friends like this, putting an embarrassing story out in the open was like throwing a monkey into a piranha-infested stream.)

"Marc, thanks, I can wear this the next time I take on Mike Tyson."

"Monette has one just like it," Michael joked.

"Michael, please, I'm proud of my status as a hermaphrodite," Monette countered. "Okay, okay, this one's from me." She pushed a large, flat object in front of my place at the table.

"A chalkboard! Oh, Monette! How did you know!"

"Just open it, smart aleck," Monette warned me.

It was a two-by-three-foot blowup of my genitals, as anyone possessing an Internet connection has seen.

"Gee, Monette. You know I'll get you back for this. Double. You wouldn't treat me like this, any of you, if I weren't in this wheelchair," I said, doing my best Joan Crawford impression from *What Ever Happened to Baby Jane?*

"BUT Y'ARE, BLANCHE, Y'ARE!" all three of them shouted back in unison.

"Okay, okay, this one is from Michael and me," Monette said, handing me a small box no more than two inches square.

"I know what it is," I shouted. I rattled the box near my ear. "It's either a brown recluse spider or a black widow in a really bad mood!"

"Don't shake it too hard," Monette blurted out and grabbed my hand. "I want to be out of the room before it detonates."

I was thankful to have such twisted friends.

I peeled the paper back, opened the box, and dug through the tissue paper. As I parted the last of the crumpled paper inside, I could hear a sharp intake of breaths around me.

It was a key. Not to a car, because it didn't have the telltale logo of the make embedded in the key design. The key to a lock? But where?

"A chastity belt?" I guessed.

"On you?" Michael laughed. "It would be unnecessary."

I couldn't figure it out.

"Apartment 19F, on Eighth Avenue and Eighteenth Street," Michael said matter-of-factly.

I was still confused.

"An apartment? But I have one on the Yupper East Side."

"Well, now you have a new one and it's in Chelsea. In a new building," Michael replied.

"But, but, I don't have the money for something that nice . . . to rent or to buy," I protested. "I sold the car Michael illegally shipped to me from Berlin and saved the money, but it's not enough, guys."

"It is now." Michael smiled, then lit up a huge cigar.

"But, but," I stammered as my eyes welled up with tears. It was impossible. "How?"

"For Christ's sake, it's not like *I* paid for it!" Michael whined, his dander rising because human emotions were being expressed. "Compliments of George Sheffield and Allen Firstborn. Mostly George. It's in one of his buildings and he was only too happy to give you the apartment free if we gave him a certain CD. It's amazing how a simple piece of fifty-nine-cent plastic could be worth so much."

I began to blubber like a six-year-old who just had his lunch money stolen by two playground bullies.

"Oh, God, he's turning on the waterworks!" Michael complained. "Now I don't have to hear you bitch about having no heat in the winter or junkies in the hallway." He blew out a large cloud of smoke from his cigar and left the room.

Marc gave me a hug, which started me crying even more.

"Don't cry, Robert, this is a happy time."

"Marc, it's not that. You're squeezing my broken rib," I explained.

"Oh, sorry."

"Now you can leave that dump behind you. You're moving up in the world!" Monette said cheerfully.

"Please clear up a few things for me, Monette," I pleaded.

"Your wish is my command."

"So Michael blackmailed Firstborn and Sheffield?"

"Yup, he shook 'em both down. Also took the risk, too. But with what we have on the two of 'em, I don't think they'll be bothering Michael. He's also a Stark. I don't think either of them wants to tangle with Stark Pharmaceuticals."

"So he took on the risk himself, just for me!" I said.

"Don't get too teary-eyed, Robert," Monette advised me in a lowered voice. "Michael is still Michael—he took a cut of the blackmail for himself."

I snorted a little laugh that hurt like hell.

"So tell me anything else I should know, about the case, that is."

Monette paused dramatically, then began. "Well, a lot has come out since the accident. The detective now in charge of the case let me in on a few things. John Bekkman was the mastermind behind a string of art thefts dating back to 1993. It seems that a few years ago, McMillan was conducting an investigation of a burglary involving some rare Roman coins and he questioned John Bekkman as a suspect. Bekkman must have felt that Luke was getting too close for comfort, so he bribed the detective two million dollars to look the other way. McMillan took the bait and was covering for John Bekkman until last year, when he asked to be transferred to the homicide division to let things cool off a bit."

"But how does Chet Ponyweather figure into all of this? I can't see where he'd ever come in contact with Bekkman or McMillan or any of their cohorts."

"Easy, he was set up by Luke McMillan for his boss, John Bekkman."

"What?" I asked in amazement.

"John needed a way to get the Van Goghs out of the Netherlands once he stole them and Chet's shipping concern could provide it. McMillan knew that Chet was a frequent visitor to Central Park at night, so McMillan posed as an undercover police officer, made advances to Chet and arrested him on an indecency charge. He threatened to expose his dick-smoking episode to his wife. Chet complied."

"Just fantastic," I said.

"The rest of John's co-conspirators really were former cops and they supplied the muscle, the equipment and their knowledge of alarm systems and police and forensic procedures to stay several steps ahead of the law. All of John's henchmen have been rounded up, but alas, the Van Goghs are still missing. Bekkman stashed them somewhere safe and who knows if they'll ever turn up. Oh, the reason Bekkman was living across from the Metropolitan Museum was because he was planning a major break in there. He was studying everything about the museum from security to building layouts and points of entry . . . the police discovered his copious notes when they drilled his apartment safe open. It's all over the news."

"So who tried to run me down . . . more than once?"

"That," Monette sighed, "we may never know. Probably Chet Ponyweather, someone from Frank Addams, Addams's IPO. brokerage firm, or Sheffield. I can say for sure that it wasn't Bekkman, McMillan or any of their gang because they preferred to bump people off quietly."

"Chloroforming them, mainly because their victims were big and strong," I added.

"In Cody and Eric's case, yes, but in yours, I think it was a quiet form of murder. No loud bangs, no noisy struggles or anything that could attract attention. Plus, they often used chloroform to knock out security guards while breaking into museums, art galleries or private apartments. Oh yes, one final thing: I used the photos of my boss, Hardcourt, to get him to forget about me putting that thyme on the extinct list, and to give me a nice little raise. And they all lived happily every after, the end."

22

You Can't Go Home Again—But Who Wants To?

A month and a half later, I was well on my way to recovery. I had outgrown the cane and was walking miles on my own. The hip still hurt when I spread my legs wide, but as Michael suggested, "That's a situation that you shouldn't face too often." Marc was with me the entire time, helping me, pushing me, and packing for me. My new apartment seemed like a palace to me, the 840 square feet feeling like Versailles. The view was not too bad. My apartment looked west and I could actually see bits and pieces of the Hudson River between the buildings that blocked a good part of my view. But I didn't care. It was mine, and I could afford the co-op fees with my meager salary.

And the big day came. Time to say goodbye to the old life and welcome to the new. I asked Marc to wait downstairs for me while I locked up my old apartment for the last time. I walked around the old dump, actually feeling like I was going to miss it in my own perverse way. Despite its size, despite the lack of heat in winter and overabundance in summer, it was the place I had spent a lot of my life and where a lot of memories were made. But it was time to move on, to grow.

And so I closed the door on the sordid apartment that I had called home for over a decade and I headed down the steps of my building to catch a cab with Marc to my new co-op in Chelsea. Things were actually getting better in my life. Sometimes in life, the little guy wins. You just gotta learn to hang in there and believe, believe, believe and have great friends who would do anything for you.

Of course, a little blackmail certainly helps things along.